By Jonathan Valin

EXTENUATING CIRCUMSTANCES

CIRCUMSTANCES

Jonathan Valin

A DELL BOOK

Published by
Dell Publishing
a division of
Bantam Doubleday Dell Publishing Group, Inc.
666 Fifth Avenue
New York, New York 10103

ISBN: 0-440-20630-8

Reprinted by arrangement with Delacorte Press

Printed in the United States of America

Published simultaneously in Canada

August 1990

10 9 8 7 6 5 4 3 2 1

OPM

To Katherine

1

. . . .

The Lessing house was on Riverside Drive in Covington, almost directly across the Ohio River from the stadium. I knew it was across from the stadium because I could hear the afternoon baseball crowd grumbling in the distance, like an army of men talking fitfully in their sleep. I couldn't see the stadium itself, or much of anything on the Ohio side. The midsummer heat had raised a mist on the river, making the crowd noises drifting over the water seem detached, dreamlike. It could have been the Styx—the distant welter, the voices of the doomed. It could also have been the Ohio River on a hot, humid July afternoon with a baseball game in progress. It was a day to make you a little soft in the brain.

What I could see, had no trouble seeing, was a pretty French Quarter house on a small rise above the street where I had parked. A flagstone terrace dotted with cane furniture. A row of French windows in a white stucco wall. A second-story veranda, railed in wrought iron with a second row of French windows opening onto it. Two people were sitting on the terrace, a man and a woman looking in opposite directions, like drawings on a jelly glass. Neither one of them was looking at me.

I hied my way up a short flight of stone steps. The man turned toward me. He was too fat to be wearing the blue polo shirt he had on without a bra. He had a long, dour, jowly face that drooped down his neck like dough from a hook. His brown crew-cut hair was chopped level on top and mowed to about a half an inch height, like a fescue lawn. I put his age at about thirty.

The fat man trained his dark eyes on me savagely, as if I'd been dragged up the stairs by the cat. The girl continued to look off into space. She was very pretty and very young, no more than twenty-five, with the fragile, frozen, doting face of an enamel shepherdess— all porcelain and gold, with just the faintest hints of pale blue and pink in her eyes and mouth. She wore a fluffy tennis outfit that made her glow in the sun.

"Are you the detective?" the fat man said irritably.

"That's me. Harry Stoner."

"Janey? The detective is here." The man looked toward the girl in the tennis outfit. His voice, which had sounded hard and officious to me, turned sugary and coaxing. I wondered if Janey was the kind of girl whom everyone addressed that way, like a favorite child.

Janey turned her head slowly toward us, and I saw that she'd been crying. The silver tear streaks made her delicate white face even prettier. The fat man ducked his head unhappily, as if he couldn't stand to see her in misery.

"This is Mr. Stoner," he said under his breath.

Janey blinked once and wiped her eyes with both hands. Her fingernails were almond-shaped and painted a pearly pink.

"Hello," she said in a childlike voice, and forced a smile. The smile faded instantly, and she looked off again, abstractedly, into the distant mist of the river.

"Janey is Ira's wife," the fat man said categorically, as if he was reminding her too.

"Are you the one who called me?" I asked him.

"Yes. I'm Len Trumaine. Ira Lessing's partner."

"And Ira is?"

The girl's eyes welled again with tears. "Gone," she said plaintively, and Len Trumaine winced. "Ira's gone."

Janey Lessing led us into the French Quarter house, down a hall lined with framed Impressionist prints that lit up the walls like rays of sunlight coming through small, high windows. Len Trumaine eyed me nervously, then looked straight ahead at Janey's tiny, skirted ass and pale enamel legs, as if she were his kid at the zoo and he was afraid to let her too far out of his sight. Eventually we came to a living room. A plump white couch, bracket-shaped, sat in front of a polished marble fireplace, with a fiery Rothko blazing above it. We settled there.

"You want a drink?" Trumaine said to me. I shook my head. "Well, I could use a drink. Janey?"

She shook her head, no. Trumaine walked over to a brass liquor cart and poured himself a very stiff scotch. He'd almost drained the glass by the time he sat down on the couch. The liquor made his face flush and brought out a thick sweat on his forehead.

"You're sweating, Len," Janey said gruesomely.

Trumaine laughed lamely. "Yeah, well, I sweat when I'm nervous, Janey. You know that." He turned to me with a weak smile. "Janey and I have known each other since we were kids. We grew up together." He said it by way of excuse, as if he didn't want to leave the impression that he was run by the girl, although that was the impression I was beginning to get.

Len Trumaine swallowed the rest of his scotch in a

gulp and set the tumbler down on a glass coffee table. "I guess you're wondering why we called you."

"About Mr. Lessing's disappearance, I assume."

Trumaine flushed again. "I forgot Janey told you that. It's about Ira all right."

"He's been gone for two days," Janey blurted out.

"Two days isn't very long," I said.

The girl's face turned red, as if I'd insulted her. "Something's happened to him!" she shrieked.

The shrillness of Janey Lessing's voice startled me, as if she'd thrown a piece of crystal at my feet.

"What makes you think something's happened to your husband?"

"I just know," she said with the same piercing certainty.

"There are all sorts of reasons why a man might drop out of sight for a short time."

The girl gave me a furious look, as if she had her heart set on tragedy, as if she usually got what her heart was set on. Trumaine quickly stepped in.

"Janey is right to be worried. Ira is a man of habit. He doesn't just disappear for days on end."

I turned toward Trumaine. "You said that you and he were partners?"

"We run a plastics company on Madison, here in Covington. Well, I run it. Ira has a number of other responsibilities."

"Such as?"

"He's a city commissioner, for one."

"That's like a councilman?"

Trumaine nodded. "Ira comes from one of the city's oldest families. The Lessings have been on the commission for decades."

"And when exactly did he disappear?"

"He left this house on the evening of the Fourth," Janey Lessing said, suddenly taking an interest in the conversation. "We'd been watching the fireworks on the terrace, and when they were over Ira said that he would be driving back to the office for a few hours."

"Did he say why he was going to the office?"

"Business, of course."

"Commissioner business or plastics business?"

The girl looked flustered. "What difference does it make what kind of business? My husband drove away on Sunday night and never came back."

She fixed her eyes on me as if she expected me to produce Ira Lessing on the spot.

"Mrs. Lessing," I said, "I'm not a magician. I need information to do my job."

"But I don't know what kind of business Ira had to do!" she cried. "I don't know about his business!" Tears welled up again in her hazel eyes, and she covered her face with her hands.

Trumaine hopped to his feet, giving me an ugly, sidelong glance. "Janey, it's going to be all right. Believe me, honey, we'll find him."

"Why did this happen, Len?" she said behind her hands.

Len petted her head. "You should go lie down," he said gently. "I'll handle this."

The girl got up as bidden and walked out of the room without giving me a glance. Trumaine stared after her with something a lot more self-interested than concern for a friend.

"You didn't have to be so tough on her," he said, turning to me.

"I wasn't being tough. I was doing my job."

"Well, do your job a little more tactfully from now

on, at least around Janey. Ira means everything to her.
I would think you could see that for yourself." Trumaine sank into a white chair opposite me and wiped
his sweaty brow. "I realize that Janey may appear to be
. . . an alarmist. But the truth is that it is completely
out of character for Ira to disappear like this, without
leaving word. Ira's compulsive. He does everything by
a timetable. He wants everything in its place, if you
see what I mean."

"I've met the wife."

Trumaine scowled weakly.

"Has Lessing made any enemies? Through the commission or through your business?"

"God, no. Everyone likes Ira. He's a genuinely decent, extremely charitable man."

There wasn't a trace of irony in his voice, although
there obviously should have been, considering how he
felt about the missus.

"He doesn't play around, does he? With other
women?"

Trumaine looked shocked. "He's got Janey," he said,
as if she were first prize in the lottery. "Why would he
do that?"

"Stranger things have happened."

2

I got Trumaine to drive me over to the plastics plant
on Madison so I could look at Ira Lessing's office. It
took him about ten minutes to work his way uptown,
through the maze of Covington's one-way streets, thick
with summer litter and summer haze. The shop stood
out distinctly in a run-down block of crumbling
storefronts—a freshly constructed concrete building
painted bright pink, with a pale blue awning running
the length of the facade, like the ribbon on a child's
Easter hat.

"The paint scheme was Ira's idea," Trumaine said.
"Ira and Janey's. To spruce the place up."

"Did it help business?"

Trumaine grunted. "It didn't hurt as much as I
thought it would. Actually, he could paint it in stripes
for all the customers care. It's the Lessing name that
makes the business go. And the product, of course."

Trumaine parked his red Volvo in a car lot beside
the pink building. The spaces were numbered 1 to 20
on the tarmac, and the first two numbers had names
stenciled beneath them—RESERVED FOR MR. LESSING, RE-
SERVED FOR MR. TRUMAINE. A tall fence surrounded the
lot, topped with barbed wire and anchored in the walls
of the shop.

"That's a helluva fence," I said as we got out of the
car.

Trumaine shrugged. "Ira didn't believe in taking
chances."

I tugged at the fencing with my right hand, making it ring up and down its length. "What did he drive, a Rolls-Royce?"

"Actually, he got a new car in May. A Beemer 325i."

"Pink and blue?"

Trumaine glared at me. "Silver and black."

"Did he take the car with him on the night of the Fourth?"

"As far as I know, yes. Anyway, it's disappeared too."

It was so hot on the street that we both broke into sweats before we could make it around the side of the building and through the entry door of Lessing & Trumaine Plastics. Inside, the air was icy cold. A pink-cheeked secretary with horn-rim glasses chained to her ears and a hairdo like a bronzed shoe sat at a desk in back of a small reception area. She smiled warmly at Len Trumaine.

"Howdy, boss," she said in a nervous, jangly voice. "Still burning hot out there?"

"Like Hades," Trumaine said, mopping his brow with one hand and digging at his blue polo shirt with the other. "Millie, this is Mr. Stoner. He's going to help us with our problem."

"Welcome to you," Millie said. "I sure hope you find Mr. L. quick. Things are starting to pile up around this place."

Trumaine shivered against something colder than the air-conditioning. "I suppose you should know that Ira signs the checks here. If we don't find him by Friday, I don't know how anybody's going to get paid this week—including you."

"Maybe he lit out for Vegas," Millie said playfully, "with the company funds."

"Does he like to gamble?" I asked her.

She threw her hand at me. "I'm just kidding. Mr. L.'s a real straight shooter. He don't gamble and he don't drink. He's a gentleman."

Trumaine guided me past Millie into Lessing's office. Like his home, the room was immaculately clean and expensively furnished in pale oak. There were several Rothkos on the walls, no advertisements for the business. But then it was already clear that Lessing was selling class, caste, and connections and not just plastics. The papers on the desk in the middle of the room were arrayed like sheet music, everything neatly piled in squares. Two framed photographs sat on opposite ends of the desk. One was Janey Lessing, in a riding outfit. The other was a picture of a blond man in his early thirties with a pale, handsome, delicately featured face, like a Pre-Raphaelite prince with a crew cut. I picked up the picture of the man. In the photo he was wearing a tuxedo coat, dress shirt, and black bow tie.

"Who's this?"

Trumaine glanced at it. "That's Ira, at some occasion or other."

"He keeps his own picture on the desk?" I said with a laugh.

Trumaine grunted. "So he's a little vain."

"That's reassuring. I was beginning to think he was too good to be true." I glanced at the discrete piles of papers on the desk. "It certainly doesn't look like anyone was working here recently."

Len Trumaine permitted himself a small laugh. "With Ira it would be hard to tell. He's compulsively neat. Been that way since I met him."

"How long have you and he known each other?"

Although I'd asked the question innocently, Trumaine didn't take it that way. He pinked a little and trimmed up his waistline, as if, next to the compulsively neat Mr. Lessing, I'd made him feel particularly fat and sloppy.

"I met him in college," he said stiffly. "We roomed together at Vanderbilt. In fact, I was the one who introduced him to Janey—on a trip home."

"Where's home?"

"Louisville. Janey's my cousin, twice removed. Our families have lived across the street from each other since we were kids."

"You and Lessing went into business after the marriage?"

Trumaine nodded.

"You seem to have done all right in the big city."

"I've made a go of this company," he said with pride. "And Ira knows it. He'd have a hard time replacing me."

"Has that been discussed recently?"

"Not at all." Trumaine flushed red. "I'm going to have to get used to your way of talking, Stoner. You're blunt."

I sat down behind Lessing's desk. There were no signs of work or wear—no quill of dulled pencils in the quartz canister, no trailing circles of ink on the desk blotter where someone tried out a pen for the first time or the last, no script impression on the memo pad where Lessing had jotted down a note and torn off the top page. The man was more than neat—he was invisible.

I lifted a letter from the top of one of the squared-up piles of correspondence. It was a purchase order from a supply house dated the second of July—the Friday before the weekend of the Fourth. There was nothing ominous about it, nothing that would have required a midnight trip to the office.

Trumaine glanced nervously at his wristwatch. "I think I should phone Janey. I don't like the idea of her being at that house alone. I mean a call might come in—"

"You go on back," I said. "I'll catch a cab and meet you at the house."

"I'm starting to get nervous," Len Trumaine said as he walked over to the door. "Maybe we should contact the cops."

"You haven't done that already?" I said with surprise.

He shook his head.

"Why?"

"Janey," Trumaine said. "The thought of having to deal with so many strangers all at once terrifies her. And then, if something should go wrong, the publicity would be awful. Reporters, TV crews. I'm sure the Lessing family feels the same way."

"They know about the disappearance?"

"Janey and Meg Lessing, Ira's mother, are very close."

"Well, I think they better change their minds about the cops," I told him, "especially if Janey is right. She seems awfully damn sure that something has happened to her husband."

"I'll talk to them," he promised.

3

. . . .

I spent about an hour going through the neat piles of
paper on Lessing's desk. The only nonbusiness items I
found were two canceled checks—one for fifty dollars
and one for ninety dollars—dated June 3, and made out
to the Lighthouse Drug Rehabilitation Clinic on Monmouth Street in Covington. Lessing had paper-clipped
them to the Sunday page of his daily calendar, as if
they were important. They looked like charitable do-
nations, but I took them with me anyway.

In the icy anteroom bronze-haired Millie was bent
over a word processor at her desk. She glanced at me as
I came out of Lessing's office. The yellow computer
screen reflecting in her glasses made it look as if she
had TV sets for eyes.

"Find anything interesting?" she asked.

"Not much."

I pulled up a chair and sat across from her. She
turned off her computer, and the TV sets in her glasses
went out with a blink. In spite of the chained horn-
rims and the prison matron's hairdo, Millie wasn't
nearly as old as she dressed. Early thirties, at best. I
had the feeling that it flattered some officious bone in
her body to look the part of a secretary, even if it was
the secretary from a forties melodrama.

"You mind talking to me about Mr. Lessing?" I
asked.

She smiled encouragingly. "Not a bit. I'd do anything to help Mr. L. or the missus."

"You like him, don't you?"

"I like him a lot," Millie said. "He's a sweet man and real well organized. I like Mr. T. too. But he can get cross when things go wrong. Mr. L. don't have a cross bone in his body. He's always so kind."

"Do you know if he was working on something special this past week?"

"Don't think so. Truth is he was only in the one time last week, on Friday. To sign the checks."

"So he spent the week away from the office?"

"I guess you could say that," Millie said. "But then he don't spend much time here, anyway. What with his commission meetings at the Court House, he only comes in three, four times a week normally."

"The commission takes up that much of his time?"

"Guess it must," Millie said. "It's been like that since I come to work here three years ago. Mr. T. handles the everyday stuff. Mr. L. comes in for meetings and to sign checks."

"Your boss didn't have a problem with drugs or alcohol, did he?"

Millie gave me a look. "Of course not. What makes you say such a thing?"

"I found two checks on his desk made out to a drug rehabilitation clinic."

Millie laughed. "You must mean the Lighthouse."

"That's the name all right. Why is that funny?"

" 'Cause Mr. L. ain't no patient there. That's just a charity he contributes to. In fact, he had a lot to do with starting the place up—him and Mr. Geneva. I think Mr. L. paid for the lease right out of his own pocket."

"Your boss must be a generous man."

"He's got a soft spot for street kids." She scowled as if she didn't share the same weakness.

I got up from the chair. "This guy Geneva you mentioned, where could I find him?"

"At the Court House," Millie said. "He's on the commission too. Mr. Don Geneva."

I started for the door.

"You don't really think something has happened to Mr. L., do you?" Millie called out.

"I don't know, Millie. Probably not."

"I hope you're right," she said, looking concerned. "There just ain't enough like him to go around. Most men are out for what they can get." She raised her ring finger and waved her wedding ring at me as evidence.

I caught a taxi on Madison and had the cabbie drive me through the boiling, smoggy heat to the Court House on Fifth Street. It was a three-story stone fortress with barred casements and balled turrets and a general air of ugly utility, like a Protestant orphanage. The information carrel inside the lobby was deserted. In fact, most of the first floor had emptied out for lunch. The only sounds came from the wall fans, buzzing on their consoles, and a few typewriters clicking away behind pebbled-glass doors.

I walked across the lobby to a staircase where a blue-jacketed security guard sat dozing on a stool. A Turfway Racing Form lay at his feet, flapping gently in the breeze from the fans. I made enough noise as I approached to wake him up. He resettled his Sam Browne around his tubby gut and gave me a rancorous look, as if he'd caught *me* napping.

"Can you point me to the commissioners' offices?" I asked.

"Ain't no one there," the cop said. "Most folks eat lunch this time of day."

"Let's pretend I already ate."

"Upstairs. Second floor." He jerked his thumb at the staircase above his head as if he was showing me the gate.

There was a directory on the wall at the top of the staircase with each of the commissioners' names listed on it, followed by an office number. Ira Lessing was 210. Don Geneva, 216.

I tried 210, but it was locked tight. I made a mental note to ask Len about getting me a key to the place, then walked down to 216. The door to Geneva's office was wide open. Inside, a well-dressed blond man in his early thirties was sitting at an oak desk, feet up, holding a sandwich in his right hand and a *Wall Street Journal* in his left. I would have bet that he was a lawyer. He had that look about him, as if he had the world by the balls.

"Help you?" the man said as I walked in.

"You can if you're Don Geneva."

The man pointed with his sandwich at the placard on the desk in front of him, and I caught a whiff of bologna. The placard read "Don Geneva, City Commissioner."

"Your name is?" Geneva said, taking a bite of the sandwich.

"Stoner. I'd like to talk to you about one of your colleagues, Ira Lessing."

"You a friend of Ira's?"

"I'm working for the family."

Geneva chewed on that for a second. "I'm pretty close to Ira and Janey, and I don't recall hearing your name."

Now, I was sure he was a lawyer. "Len Trumaine hired me this afternoon."

Geneva smirked when I mentioned Trumaine. "Plastics stuff?" he said, as if Len and plastics were the least interesting things in the world.

"No. I'm a private detective. Mr. Lessing has been missing since Sunday night, and the family's hired me to try to find him."

Geneva's mouth fell so wide open I could see the bologna on his molars. He dropped the newspaper on his desk and the sandwich on the newspaper, sat up in his chair, and gawked at me.

"If this is a joke . . ."

"It's not a joke, Mr. Geneva."

Geneva put his hands on the desk and pushed himself back in his chair, as if he was going to stand up. But he didn't stand up. He just sat there, looking stunned. "Chrissake," he said in a shocked voice. "You got ID?"

I showed him the photostat of my license. He stared at it blankly, then handed it back to me.

"Maybe you could answer a few questions?" I asked.

"Sure," he said, still looking stunned.

"When's the last time you saw Mr. Lessing?"

"Here. On Friday. At the commission meeting."

"Was anything special discussed at this meeting? Any project that Lessing was involved in?"

"No. It was a slow day, even for July. We had a couple of zoning disputes and building-code violations. Nothing that anyone really cared about, if that's what you mean."

"Did you talk to Lessing?"

"Of course I did," Geneva said. "We're good friends."

"Did he mention any plans for the weekend? Any business plans?"

Geneva thought about it for a second. "No. He said he and Janey were going to watch the fireworks on Sunday, like they do every year. He asked what Jeanne and I were planning for the Fourth. You know, small talk."

"Did he seem at all preoccupied to you? Distracted or depressed?"

"Ira depressed?" Geneva said in a scoffing voice. "Ira is one of the most upbeat men I've ever met. He's always positive. That's just his nature. A decent, positive man. Just ask anyone here at the Court House. Anyone in Covington. Hell, everybody likes Ira."

He got a worried look on his face, as if he was considering what he had just said. "Christ, it's awful to think that something could have happened to him."

It surprised me a little that a guy like Geneva, with his razor-cut good looks and snotty air of self-possession, could get shaken up about anything other than the loss of a retainer. Apparently Lessing had made an impression on him. And that impressed me.

"Lessing didn't mention a place called the Lighthouse at the meeting, did he?"

Geneva half smiled, as if the name was familiar to him. "Why do you ask?"

"He left some checks on his desk made out to it."

"That's normal. Sam Kingston, the director, is always phoning Ira up for an extra buck."

"The Lighthouse is one of Lessing's projects?"

Geneva nodded. "It's a clinic on Monmouth for teenage drug abusers. Ira started the thing by personally soliciting contributions. He even got me to pitch in. Eventually we got the commission to fund the place. It's a step toward cleaning that damn street up."

"What's so special about Monmouth?"

"There's a good deal of drug trafficking and prostitution around the bars there. And that upsets a lot of people, not just Ira. Of course nobody did anything but complain until Ira came along. He paid the bills for the clinic out of his own pocket for almost a year. Still pays a few, when the grant money runs low."

"Why so generous?" I asked.

"Ira thinks the city should look after the street kids —and all the other folks who haven't had the advantages that we've had." Although he said it with the sort of light irony that you'd expect from a guy like him, the irony was mixed with something respectful and fond.

"He sounds like an old-fashioned do-gooder," I said, smiling.

"That's exactly what he is," Geneva said. "Ira can bore you to death with facts and figures. I mean, he's a stickler for detail. But under the bow tie and pressed shirt, he's got a heart of gold and everyone knows it."

His face fell. "Look, if there's anything I can do to help find him, don't hesitate to call me. Here or at home. I really mean that."

"I'm sure the Lessings will appreciate your offer."

"I just hope it's a false alarm."

4

· · · · · · · · · · · · · · ·

Before returning to the Lessing house I caught a cab to
the Lighthouse Clinic on upper Monmouth Street. On
the way uptown I took a look at the bars that Geneva
had mentioned—little brick boxes, with light bulbs
flashing around their doors and sandwich signs on the
sidewalks advertising the most beautiful girls in Kentucky, all nude, all the time. And of course there was
the street traffic that had apparently upset Lessing.
Sixteen- and seventeen-year-old girls in Madonna-
ware, with their spikey hair spray-painted purple and
their eyes made up like Halloween masks. Twenty-
year-olds in leather minis and tube tops, their breasts
oozing out of their bodices like squibs of toothpaste.
They schooled together in groups, according to their
ages, wandering up and down the blocks in front of
the bars, occasionally darting out into the street, getting swallowed up by a passing car and speeding off.
I'd seen that kind of thing so many times before in so
many different cities that the bars and the whores
seemed like part of the urban landscape now, like fire-
plugs and phone lines. I guessed Lessing had seen
them differently.

The Lighthouse was a half mile north of the red-
light district, a brick storefront in the middle of a com-
mercial block. The front window had been boarded
over with painted plyboard, and a sign had been hung
above the door picturing a lighthouse. A teenage girl
was sitting in the doorway, looking very stoned and

very lost. As I got out of the cab she walked over and panhandled me for change.

"Why don't you go inside?" I said to her, pointing at the building.

"Why don't you get fucked?" she said, stalking off. "I ain't ready to be saved."

Judging from the thinness of her arms and the sallowness of her complexion, I gave her a few more weeks. Then she'd be ready for anything.

I walked through the open door into a reception room filled with folding chairs. A half-dozen spaced-out kids sat there, nodding off. There was an unmanned secretary's desk at the rear of the waiting area, with a sign on its corner saying "Counseling." A long aisle ran from the back of the waiting area to a pair of swinging doors with the word "Clinic" printed on them. Behind that door a kid was screaming holy murder. The junkies on the folding chairs didn't seem to notice, but it got my attention, all right. After a few minutes the screaming subsided into sobs, then stopped altogether. A young nurse, looking ashen-faced, came through the swinging doors and up the aisle. She sat down at the counseling desk.

I walked over to her.

"You all right?" I asked.

She nodded slowly, as if she were making up her mind about it at that very moment. "Yeah, I'll be all right. Can I help you?"

"I'd like to talk to Sam Kingston."

She glanced over her shoulder at the swinging doors. "Sam's busy at the moment."

"I heard."

"Some kid freaked out on T's and B's. Sam's talking

him down. He shouldn't be too much longer if you want to wait."

I sat on one of the folding chairs, next to a kid who smelled like a clothes hamper. A few minutes went by, then a stocky, bearded black man in a doctor's frock coat came through the swinging doors. He walked over to the waiting area and sat down heavily on the corner of the nurse's desk.

"What's next, I wonder?" he said, rubbing savagely at his thick black beard.

"Sam?" the nurse said. "That fellow's been waiting to talk to you." She pointed at me.

The man turned his head toward me and held out his hand. "I'm Sam Kingston. How can I help you?"

"My name is Stoner, Dr. Kingston," I said, shaking with him. "Could I talk to you for a few minutes?"

"You a narc, Mr. Stoner?"

I smiled at his savvy. "No. A private detective. I'm working for the Lessing family."

The name Lessing made Sam Kingston straighten up

"Come on back to the office," he said.

The office was nothing more than a glassed-in carrel in one corner of the clinic. The Hippocratic oath was hung like a stitched motto above a tiny desk and chair. The only other furnishing was a stained Mr. Coffee machine sitting on a plastic table.

"What exactly do you do for Ira?" Kingston said, pouring two cups of coffee and handing one to me.

"Right now, what I'm doing is looking for him."

"Did you try at his office or over at the Court House?"

"He's disappeared, Dr. Kingston. Since Sunday night no one has seen or heard from him."

Kingston sat down on his desk chair, slopping a little coffee on the floor. "Seriously?"

"I'm afraid so."

Kingston set the coffee cup on the corner of his desk and stared at me with concern. "I sure hope nothing's happened to him. It might sound corny, but the guy is a saint. Without him none of this would exist. Not the Lighthouse or half a dozen other charities and halfway houses around town. My God, he's put over ten thousand of his own dollars in this place alone. And if we run short or some kid needs money for special treatment, all you have to do is ask Ira. I don't know how much he's handed out over the years. All you have to do is ask."

"You haven't seen or heard from him this week or weekend, have you?"

"I talked to him on Saturday afternoon," Kingston said.

"What did he say?"

"The usual things. He asked how we were doing, if there was anything we needed."

"Did you need anything special?"

"Money," Kingston said with an embarrassed laugh. "We always need money. The Lighthouse is funded by the commission now. But, in spite of the dole, we're perpetually short. Ira mails us a monthly check to help defray costs. And of course we're always sending local kids to him for handouts—to help get them started in the program."

I asked Kingston the same thing I'd asked Don Geneva: "Why is he so charitable to street kids?"

"Because he's a good man," Kingston said thoughtfully, as if he'd asked himself the same question many times before. "I mean I've talked to him about it. Sometimes you can't help thinking you're taking advantage of a guy who's that generous. But he says it's something he needs to do. He has more money than he can use, and he doesn't have any children of his own. He just wants to help kids."

I reached into my coat and pulled out the two canceled checks I'd found in Ira's calendar.

"I found these on Lessing's desk. They might have meant something special to him. Do they mean anything to you?"

Kingston reached out and took the checks. "They look like Ira's usual doles—to get kids started in the drug rehab program."

"Nothing unusual about them?"

"Not that I can see. I could have our bookkeeper, Marty Levine, examine them if you want to leave them with me. She's out on vacation this week, but she should be back next Monday."

"All right," I said. "Just don't lose track of them, Doc, okay?"

Kingston pulled open the drawer of his desk and laid them gently inside, as if he was burying a pet.

5

. . . .

It was close to four when I finished with Kingston. I caught a cab on Monmouth and had the cabbie drive me back to Riverside Drive. As we turned onto the street I spotted a rusting blue-and-white Cincinnati police cruiser parked beneath the graceful French Quarter house. At first I thought that Trumaine must have talked Janey Lessing into calling the cops, although why she'd called the Cincinnati cops rather than the Covington department was a mystery. But as I paid the cabbie I saw Trumaine come out the front door with a plainclothes detective beside him. Even at a distance I recognized the detective—his name was Art Finch and he was on the CPD homicide squad.

"Christ," I said to myself.

When Trumaine spotted me on the sidewalk, he began waving his arms wildly, as if the fine, delicate house behind him had suddenly caught fire in the July sun. Despite Trumaine's arm-waving, I took my time climbing the stairs. I don't run toward tragedies unless I can do something to prevent them. And in this case it looked like I was too late to do anything at all.

Finch nodded at me as I came up onto the terrace. He was a big man with a stolid, brick-red face and sun-streaked reddish-blond hair. By habit and temperament, his expression was always sullen. Len Trumaine's face told all.

"They found Ira's car," he said in a stricken voice. "My God, my God."

I turned to Finch. "Where?"

"In Queensgate, in the Terminal lot."

"Was he inside?"

Finch shook his head, no. "Lots of blood, though."

Trumaine literally shrank back out of the burning sunlight into the shade of the veranda. "I think I'm going to be sick," he said hoarsely. "I don't believe this is happening." His head fell heavily to his chest.

I walked over to him and put a hand on his shoulder. His polo shirt was slick to the touch, and the flesh underneath it felt like bagged ice. "Try to get hold of yourself," I said softly. "Janey's going to need you."

Trumaine jerked his head up as if I'd slapped him, bumping the back of his skull against the stucco wall of the house. His face contracted with pain and he said, "Ow," before he could check himself. It was just the sort of indignity that had been visited upon the poor, overweight son-of-a-bitch all his life. He knew it, and he knew that I knew it, with a fat man's cruel sense of injured vanity. He reached back to rub his head, his lips trembling.

"Goddamnit," he said.

"Go on in the house. Clean up."

"I'll be all right," he said, fighting to control his voice.

He started through the door, then turned back to me.

"Janey's out with Meg. She doesn't know."

"Are you anxious to tell her?"

He shook his head violently.

"Then look after yourself for a while," I told him.

Once Trumaine had gone inside, I asked Finch for the details.

"The car had been parked there for a couple of

days," he said. "Somebody at the Terminal got curious and took a look inside. Then they called us. We found a bunch of credit cards piled up on the front seat and this man Lessing's wallet. There was dried blood all over the front seat, on the roof of the car, and in the back too."

"You haven't found a body?"

"Not yet." He glanced at the front door of the house. "We're going to need that guy to make an identification on the personal stuff. You think he can handle it?"

"Better him than the wife."

"Okay. I'll go down to the car and radio in. You get him and meet me down there. And don't take too long. People are dying in this heat."

I found Trumaine in the living room, with a bottle of scotch in his hand and a blasted look on his face. I didn't have the heart to tell him that this was just the beginning. That he'd strayed into a piece of machinery that could eat him alive—and Janey Lessing too. The pitiless, piddling, inexact machinery of justice.

"They're going to need you to identify the car and Lessing's belongings."

"I don't want to do it," he said flatly.

"It's you or Janey."

Trumaine half smiled, as if in the back of his mind he'd already known it would come to that. He took a big swig of scotch, then got to his feet, digging fecklessly at his loose blue shirttail.

"I ought to call a few of Ira's friends. Somebody should be here when Janey and Meg get back. I'd better call my sister, Fran, too, in Louisville."

"Make your calls," I said. "I'll meet you at the car."

* * *

Nobody said a word on the short, hot ride across the river to Queensgate. Trumaine stared out the side window, trying like hell to hold himself together in the boiling, fetid air of the police cruiser. It was an environment he hadn't experienced—the backseat of a police car, with its handleless doors, its windows that open a finger's width and no more, its jail smells of dirt, destitution, and fear. I'd made the trip before, and I wasn't any more comfortable than he was. Riding in the back of a cop car always made me squirm.

In the front Finch played finger games on the steering wheel. Now and then the radio squawked like a startled crow. The misty river went by us in a blur of bridge struts and passing cars. Then we were on the expressway, in the concrete bottom of the old industrial basin. Then we were off the highway, on the worn brick border of the projects. And then we were there—at the Union Terminal, its huge half-dome looming like a band shell on a vast lawn of glaring concrete.

We'd arrived too quickly for Len Trumaine. I could see it in his face, the way his eyes and mouth dropped as if he'd been slugged, the motion of his throat as if he were trying to swallow but didn't have the spit. He needed more time to prepare himself. And for just a second, as the car pulled up in front of the old train depot plaza, I was afraid he was going to panic. But he didn't.

He got out into the shade of the front awning and looked up at the enormous Art Deco facade of the Terminal, at the huge iron clock on the mullioned windows of the half-dome. "Five o'clock," he said, as if he was fixing the hour in his mind.

Out in the lot three other police cruisers were
parked beside a silver BMW 325i. A yellow bunting of
ribbon had been strung around the car to cordon it off.
Even at that hour of the afternoon, in that heat, there
was a small crowd of people trying to catch a look.
Well-dressed clerks and shoppers from the Terminal
stores, bandy old men from the neighborhood, teenage
kids in T-shirts and ragged cutoffs. An insectile van
with a TV antenna looming from its back like a bee-
tle's wing stood beside the cruisers. A sweating news-
man was rehearsing for a Minicam operator, using the
BMW for backdrop.

"Do the newsmen have to be there?" Trumaine said
to Finch.

"I'll scare 'em off." Finch started across the lot toward the car.

Trumaine watched him closely.

"Are you all right?" I asked.

"No." He chirruped nervously, a high-pitched
squawk like the sound of the police radio.

I patted his arm. "You're doing fine."

"You think so? When I got out of the car, I was
afraid my legs wouldn't work."

"You'll make it."

"This is just the start, isn't it?" he said.

I told him the truth. "I'm afraid so."

"Oh, it's all right," he said with eerie serenity.

And I realized again that some part of him was resigned to self-sacrifice. Not even bitterly resigned to it.
But resigned to it as if it were his lot, as if it were the
price he paid for staying close to Janey Lessing. I
hoped the sacrifice was worth it, because he was showing a lot of guts and I liked him for it.

After he'd cleared the area of newsmen, Finch

waved us over to the BMW. The passenger-side door hung open, and even at a distance you could see the dark bloodstains covering the leather seat. Then you could smell the foul stench of decaying blood.

Trumaine covered his mouth and gagged. "Christ," he said, turning away.

"Is that Lessing's car?" Finch asked.

Trumaine nodded, his back to us.

Finch glanced at me uneasily. "I have some items from the car I'd like you to look at."

Trumaine waved his hand, as if he were calling time-out. After a few seconds he turned around again. "Okay," he said between his teeth. "But could we move away from the car? I don't want to get sick in front of all these people."

I walked Trumaine back to the Terminal plaza. He didn't say anything as we walked. He was too busy talking to himself. He was saying, "Dog, dog, go away." He was saying, "This can't be real." He was saying whatever it took to keep him from breaking down. A soft man trying to be strong.

When we got to the plaza, he asked me if he could go inside and get a drink of water. He walked straight through one of the revolving doors, his back bent, his face white and tormented, as if he'd taken a brutal beating. Finch came up carrying a plastic bag with a bunch of credit cards and a wallet inside it.

"They were in the car?" I asked, pointing to the contents of the bag.

He nodded. "Weird robbery, huh? Leaving all this stuff behind?"

"Does that mean you don't think it was a robbery?"

"It means I think it's weird. Period."

"Do you have any leads?"

He eyed me coldly. "Stoner, you know better than to ask that."

"It would help the family to know."

Finch looked around him, as if he didn't want to be overheard. "Someone saw a kid driving the BMW on Sunday night."

"Where?"

"In Price Hill."

"You know who the kid is?"

"We're working on it," he said vaguely.

"You don't have any idea where Lessing is, do you?"

"We're working on that too."

Len Trumaine came out of the Terminal, not looking much better than he had when he went in. There was a water stain on his shirt, above one of the fat paps on his chest. He fingered the wet spot nervously, as if it embarrassed him.

Finch opened the plastic bag and held it out to Trumaine. "It's okay to touch the stuff," he said. "It's already been dusted for prints."

Trumaine took a deep breath, reached in, and fished out a stained leather wallet. His lip curled back as he held it out in front of him. "It's Ira's, all right. Those are his initials on the inside there."

He dropped the wallet back in the bag and rubbed his hand savagely against his pants leg.

"Was Mr. Lessing in the habit of carrying large sums of money on him?" Finch said.

"He always carried a few bills. Mostly he paid for things by check."

"Do you know if he was carrying money with him on the night of the Fourth?"

"You'd have to ask Janey."

"Do you have any idea why he might have been over on this side of the river?"

Len shook his head. "He told Janey he was going to the office on Sunday night."

Finch gave him an irritated look. "I guess we'll have to talk to the wife, then."

"She's going to need a few days to recover from this," Trumaine said quickly.

Finch ignored him, signaling to a beat cop to bring one of the prowl cars around. "I guess that's it. I'll have an officer drive you home."

Len gawked at him in disbelief. "But what about Ira! What happened to Ira?"

"I think we have to assume that he was the victim of a robbery and an assault."

Trumaine looked astonished. "That's all? I mean that's all you can tell me?"

"For the time being," Finch said.

"That's not good enough. Not by a long shot."

"Take it easy, Len," I said to him.

"Don't tell me to take it easy!" he shouted. "I want to know what happened. I want to know *how* this could happen—to a decent, respectable man."

"Mr. Trumaine," Finch said, "I just can't answer that question."

"Well, I'm going to get an answer," Trumaine said angrily.

The police cruiser pulled up on the plaza.

"C'mon, Stoner," Trumaine said, piling into the backseat of the cop car.

Finch stared after him unhappily. "Try to explain to him how it works, will you?" he said to me.

"I'll try."

6

. . . .

So many cars were parked on Riverside Drive that there wasn't enough room for the police cruiser to pull up in front of the Lessing house.

"The whole family must be here," Trumaine said, staring out the window at the Mercs and BMW's lining the curbs.

"It's hard to keep a murder secret."

"Murder," he said, trying the word out for the first time. "You think Ira's dead, then?"

"I think there's a strong possibility."

"I just can't believe it. I don't think I'll be able to believe it until they find a body."

The cop let us off at the head of the drive and we walked the short block to the stairway. The mist of the river had begun to climb the cut-stone retaining walls along the Ohio's bank, trailing up the narrow cobbled street like a thin, damp fog.

"What a day for it," Trumaine said miserably. He looked at the stairway. "It's going to be awful in there."

"I'm sure Janey will take it hard."

"She'll be crazy," he said flatly. "Thank God for Meg. She'll help her through this." He turned toward me, wiping the sweat from his face with a trembling hand. "You've been a help, Stoner. I . . . I don't think I could have done this without you."

"You did the hard part," I said.

"Thanks anyway."

"You need me anymore tonight?" I said to him, hoping that he would say no.

"I think you better come up. Meg may want to talk to you about what to do. And Janey."

He hitched up his pants and started for the stairs. Reluctantly, I fell in behind him.

As we neared the top steps we began to hear the tumult inside the house. I thought of the sound of the stadium crowd that afternoon, the steady grumbling noise from across the river, rising and falling with the wind. From the terrace this sound would have been just as ambiguous if we hadn't already known its meaning.

Trumaine hesitated by the door, then pushed it open.

As he stepped inside, Janey Lessing came tearing up the hall, her beautiful face wildly anguished. She came to a stop in front of Trumaine and stared at him for a moment, with a flicker of hope in her eyes. When he ducked his chin, her eyes went dead.

"It's true, then?" she said. "What they said about Ira's car?"

Trumaine took a deep breath and nodded.

Janey started to whine—a muffled siren sound, like the noise of an electric alarm going off. She collapsed against Trumaine, burying her head in his chest and pounding on his shoulders with clenched fists, and all the time making that little electric noise. Trumaine stared at her piteously, his hands hovering above her shoulders as if he couldn't quite bring himself to touch.

The hall had filled up with people. A smart-looking woman with closely cropped white hair and a tear-

stained face came forward and lifted Janey away from
Trumaine, as if she were pulling off a frightened cat.
Her fists still clenched, the girl stared at the older
woman in horror. For a second Janey's mouth hung
open noiselessly, then it filled with an awful moan.
The woman clasped Janey to her immediately, stifling
the scream with her body and leading the girl back
down the hall.

Trumaine sobbed.

"Oh, my God," he said.

I put a hand on his shoulder and guided him toward
the living room, where the fifteen or twenty friends
and relatives were gathered. Somewhere on the upper
floor Janey Lessing began to scream like a baby in the
night. The sound of her voice sent a thrill of visible
terror through the room, making the others shift nervously where they stood or sip at drinks or begin to
cry out loud themselves. As soon as he heard Janey
shriek, Len Trumaine bolted toward a staircase on the
far side of the room and disappeared up it.

Within a matter of minutes the screaming died
away. I settled in a corner chair, feeling desperately
out of place, and waited for Trumaine or someone else
to tell me to go.

More people came to the door. Cousins, nephews,
aunts, uncles, friends. Most of them had heard the
news on TV—that Lessing's bloodstained car had been
found in Queensgate. Nobody wanted to believe it.
"Ira, of all people!" they said in stunned voices, as if
crime should never have touched him, as if his goodness made him immune. I watched them, murmuring
in groups in the middle of Lessing's handsome living
room, and knew that each of them was hoping to hear

that it had all been a mistake. Hoping that Lessing himself would come through the door.

It could happen. He didn't have to be dead. He could have been dumped somewhere after having been beaten. But I didn't believe that—not after seeing the amount of blood inside the car.

Twenty or thirty minutes went by—slowly. I saw Geneva come through the front door, a grim, abstracted look on his face. He didn't see me. After a time I got up and found my way down a short hall into a kitchen full of tin pots, Poggenpohl cabinets, and brushed-aluminum appliances. There was a phone beside the refrigerator. I picked it up and tried calling Lieutenant Al Foster at CPD to see if he could fill me in on what Finch had held back. But Foster was out of the office for the week—on assignment.

As I was standing there with the phone in my hand, the smart-looking white-haired woman who had comforted Janey walked into the kitchen. She'd been crying and her eyes were still wet with tears.

"You're Mr. Stoner, aren't you?" she said.

"Yes."

She held out her right hand. "I'm Meg Lessing, Ira's mother."

I shook with her. Under different circumstances I would have thought her attractive in a chic, sportive, well-tended way. But the terrible strain of the afternoon had put a cruel edge on her good looks. I could see it clearly in her gray eyes—a coldness that made her tears look like dew on stones. I withered a little under her gaze, feeling as much the outsider as her eyes seemed to say I was.

I asked about Janey—to break the pall.

"She's asleep, thank God. We have a doctor coming, but I don't think he'll be much help. Janey loves Ira so." Meg Lessing's voice shook for a moment, and she put a hand to her throat to steady it. "We all do. He is a very good man."

She eyed me expectantly, as if she were waiting for me to agree.

"I'm sure he is a good man," I said.

"Is there something you can tell me about . . . about what happened? I mean, Len doesn't seem to know anything at all."

"I don't think anyone knows very much at this point, Mrs. Lessing. I have been told that a boy was seen driving your son's BMW in Price Hill on the night of the Fourth."

The woman looked alarmed. "A boy? What boy?"

"The police don't like to give out names before they make an arrest. They're always cautious at this stage of an investigation."

"But I want to know the boy's name!" she said with real urgency.

I stared at her curiously. "You have someone particular in mind?"

"I just want to know where my son is," she said in a cooler voice.

I knew at once that she still thought that Ira Lessing was alive. And she knew from my reaction that I didn't.

The woman's stony look simply fell apart, as if I'd tapped her cheek with a hammer. "You think he's dead, don't you?"

I hesitated for an instant before answering, and the scattered pieces of her face flew together furiously, like a film of broken crockery run in reverse.

"You *do* think he's dead," she said accusingly, as if bad thoughts had killed him.

Trumaine walked into the room, looking worn, red-eyed, and disheveled. "What's the matter?" he said to the woman when he saw her staring icily at me.

"Mr. Stoner thinks Ira is dead."

Trumaine sighed. "Meg, nobody knows yet. Not Stoner or the police."

"Well, *I* know he's still alive. My son is still alive." She clutched at a little gold cross on her bosom.

"God would not permit anything to happen to my son," she said passionately.

Trumaine pulled her against him. "It's all right, Meg."

"I don't want that man here," Mrs. Lessing said in a hoarse whisper.

"Meg, he helped me today. He may be able to help us again."

"I don't care. We will handle this on our own, as a family. The way Tom would have handled it. The way Ira . . ." Her voice broke.

Trumaine cast an apologetic look over Meg Lessing's shoulder. "Stoner, I'm sorry."

"It's all right," I said.

And like that I was out of it.

I walked back down the hall, through the living room filled with murmuring mourners, into the blistering night. I looked back once from the street at the Lessing house, lit at every window. I felt sorry for Trumaine, for having to hold it all together. I felt sorry for Meg Lessing, for the way I'd hurt her. I felt sorry for the pretty wife. And for Lessing himself, for the terrible thing that had happened to him. But I couldn't say that I felt sorry that it wasn't my case. In fact, it had all unfolded so quickly that I hadn't really begun to think of it as a case. It seemed more like an accident that I had somehow been caught up in. And now it was police business. Now it was over.

7

. . . .

I was curious enough to follow the Lessing case in the
papers and on TV for the next few days, but not curious enough to do any investigating. I did call Art
Finch at the CPD to tell him about the checks I'd left
with Dr. Kingston at the Lighthouse. A couple of
times I toyed with the idea of calling Trumaine, but
thought better of it. He had his hands full already.

According to the media, there weren't any fresh
leads, although the Lessing name guaranteed the front
page of the *Enquirer* two days running and drew a lu-
gubrious moral from a local TV anchorman whose
specialty was excursions into the vale of tears. When
nothing new broke on the third day, the story was
moved to the local section of the papers. On the fourth
day it dropped off the tube like pie from a plate. On
the morning of the fifth day, Sunday, Len Trumaine
called me at my new apartment on Ohio Avenue—
three rooms on a first floor, with exposed brick walls
and a bay window looking out on a bleak, crowded
street.

Len sounded flustered, as if he hadn't quite figured
out what to say if I answered the phone. "You think we
could meet this afternoon, Harry? I mean if you're still
willing to talk to me after that scene with Meg."

"Mrs. Lessing was right, Len. I didn't belong there."

"She was very upset," Trumaine said quickly. "She's
still upset—with the cops and with me."

"Why you?"

"She thinks I'm not riding the police hard enough—not getting results."

"Then they haven't made any progress?"

"If they have, they're not telling me," he said miserably. "The family's posted a reward for information. And Don Geneva is organizing a citizens' group to help search for Ira. In fact, he's taken on the job of handling most of the public relations for this thing—you know, fending off the press. It's a relief, believe me."

"How's Janey taking it? Is she any better?"

Trumaine sighed. "She's stopped screaming, if that's what you mean. She's been holding her breath since Tuesday night. I don't know how much longer she can keep it in. I think she's made up her mind that Ira is dead. It really irritates Meg, who is just as convinced that he's still alive—that the police are concealing evidence, that the blood from the car is someone else's blood, that Ira has . . . I don't know, gone into hiding or something. She's pretty confused on the subject. I guess the truth is she just can't accept the possibility that he might be . . . gone."

"How can I help?" I said.

"Have a drink with me. And I'll tell you."

Around one that afternoon I drove over to Mike Fink's, one of the many riverboats-turned-restaurant moored on the Kentucky side of the river. When I arrived, Trumaine was sitting at a topside table in the striped shade of a red-and-white awning. Although he wasn't wearing the blue polo shirt, he still looked pinched and peaked by his summer shirt and golfer's slacks, but then he was the sort of man whose clothes would always look a half size too small or too large.

Out on the water, cruisers filled with sleek young partyers roared by, trailing a racket of loud laughter in their wakes. Trumaine stared after them resentfully, as if he'd forgotten how to laugh.

"They should police this area," he said bitterly. "The Coast Guard should police it and hand out speeding tickets."

"You're in a bad mood."

"You bet." He picked up his empty Tom Collins glass and signaled one of the waitresses. "Another one of these. And one for my friend."

"Has anything changed since you called?" I asked.

"Just more of the same. If the cops don't find Ira soon, I don't know what will happen." He jiggled the ice in his glass for a few seconds, gathering the nerve to make his pitch. "I'd like to hire you again, Harry, if you're available."

I couldn't say that I didn't know it was coming. "Len, I don't think that's a good idea."

"Why?" he said, looking hurt

"A couple of reasons. First, it's a police case now, and they don't much like private investigators snooping in an ongoing investigation. Second, the family doesn't want me around. And without their approval, I lose my legal excuse to butt in."

"I'm Ira's partner," he said stoutly. "Don't I have a legitimate reason to hire an investigator?"

"Yeah," I admitted, "you do."

"I want someone I trust to work on this thing. Someone who can talk to the cops."

"The cops may not talk to me, either, Len."

"I'll take that chance."

"And if it turns out that Lessing's dead?"

As I spoke the waitress arrived with the drinks. She

put the glasses down awkwardly, as if she'd been startled by what she'd overheard. Trumaine ignored her, snatching up his Tom Collins and draining half of it in a gulp.

"Christ, I'm drinking a lot," he said to himself, and swallowed the rest of the drink, as if he were proving the point. Flushing, he smacked the glass down hard on the table. "I just want this to end, Harry, even if Ira is . . . dead. At least Janey will stop holding her breath. I'm sure that's what Ira would want for her too."

It sounded like a fond hope to me from what I'd seen of Janey Lessing.

"She's very attached to him," I said cautiously.

But he didn't take it the way I'd meant it.

"Sure she's attached. Ira has been a wonderful influence on her. Janey was a very unhappy girl before they met. Neurotic, shy, totally inhibited around strangers, dominated by her father. I realize that you've only seen her at her worst, but she really did blossom when she got married. Ira made her happy."

He said this with a touch of melancholy, as if that was an achievement he admired but couldn't bring off on his own.

"Didn't you tell me that you were their matchmaker?"

Trumaine smiled wistfully. "I wanted them to get married, yes. I knew he'd be good for her. Ira's got an orderly mind, and that's something that Janey has lacked all her life—a sense of order, a sense of security. And he's a truly kind man. I mean . . . look at me. You wouldn't think a blueblood like Ira Lessing would want to be seen with a slob like me. Much less go into business with him. From the moment I met Ira in college he was a friend. He helped me through my courses; he loaned me money when I ran low; he gave my life new direction. What did I have to give him in return?" He spread his hands as if he held Janey there, like an aura. "Sure, I introduced them. He's the best friend I've ever had."

He'd worked himself up to a pitch of gratitude, helped along by the alcohol. But I'd seen him around Janey, and I knew that it must have hurt to give her away, even to a best friend.

"Please, Harry," Len Trumaine pleaded. "Help me get this thing under control."

Against my better judgment, I said I'd help.

8

. . . .

I could have waited until Monday morning to talk to the cops. But I was feeling sorry for Len Trumaine as I drove away from Mike Fink's. So instead of going home once I crossed the river, I drove north on Central Parkway, uptown through the fierce glare of the afternoon sun, to the Cincinnati Police Building on Ezzard Charles.

I found Art Finch in the Homicide bullpen on the second floor of the CPB, sitting at a battered desk, a dead cigarette butt clenched between his teeth like a carpet tack. Behind him, in a blinded window, a dusty air conditioner wheezed and rattled as if it were carrying the room on its back.

When Finch spotted me his red, sullen face bunched up miserably. "Chrissake!" he grumbled. "That guy Trumaine calls me three times a day. When he's done the mother or the wife or that commissioner, Geneva, gets on the line. Now they send you."

"They're worried." I drew a chair up to the desk and sat down. "They want Ira back. They'd like to know how long it's going to take."

"What am I, a fortune-teller? It'll take as long as it takes. I've already told them that."

"Art, the wife is close to a nervous breakdown. She needs to hear something concrete. They all do."

"Concrete, huh?" Finch sighed melodramatically. "This is a criminal investigation, Stoner."

"C'mon, Art," I said. "Stop being a prick and give

me a little something. Enough to make the Lessings happy. Enough to get them off your back."

That interested him. "No more phone calls?"

"I guarantee it."

He thought it over for a second, then tossed his hands in the air as if he were surrendering. "What the hell. We're so close as it is, I guess it won't matter. But if I hear back from the Lessings about this or see anything in the papers, you're going to be one sorry camper."

"It's that bad?"

"It ain't good." He plucked the cigarette butt from his mouth and tossed it in a tin ashtray, then leaned back in his chair. "We're pretty sure that the guy who went joyriding in Lessing's car is a kid named Terry Carnova. We got his name from some other kid who saw him on the night of the Fourth. Carnova told the second kid that the car belonged to his father. He claimed the bloodstains came from a fight he'd had with a nigger earlier that night. Criminalistics checked the stains, and they matched Lessing's blood type. The family doesn't know this yet, but we also found some bloodstained gear in the trunk."

"What kind of gear?"

"A tire iron, some jumper cables. They had Lessing's blood on them too—and some tissue."

"Christ," I said grimly. "He must've really been worked over."

"I told you it wasn't good."

"Were there any prints on this stuff?"

"On all of it. And all over the car. Just like the demented bastard didn't give a shit."

"Anything usable?"

"There was a piece of broken glass on the backseat, come out of the moon roof of the car. Criminalistics got a positive lift from it. One from a credit card too. They're Carnova's prints."

"The kid has a record, then?" I said.

"Twelve priors as a juvenile. B and E's, assault, possession. He's a typical Price Hill street kid—tough, nasty, anything for a buck."

"A JD?"

"Not anymore," Finch said with something like glee. "He turned eighteen last week."

"You figure he treated himself to a ride in Lessing's BMW for a birthday present?"

"We've got a couple theories about why he mugged Lessing. When we talk to Carnova I'll let you know for sure."

"And when will that be?"

Finch shook his head firmly, as if we'd reached the limits of his sense of obligation or expediency. "Just tell the family we're real close."

"And Lessing?"

"I'm not absolutely sure, but I don't think the news is gonna be good."

We stared at each other for a moment.

"You wouldn't have a photograph of Carnova, would you?" I asked.

Finch rummaged through a pile of papers, pulled out a Xeroxed rap sheet with a mug shot in its corner, and handed it to me. Terry Carnova was a muscular youngster with a lean, pretty, snake-eyed face and long, dirty blond hair that curled like sunlit ivy about his forehead and cheeks. He looked like an altar boy in hell.

"How could a guy like Lessing end up getting his brains bashed in by a kid like this?" I asked.

"That's the question, all right," Finch agreed.

When I got back to my apartment I phoned Len Trumaine. Finch had given me a copy of Carnova's rap sheet, and I stared at the kid's picture again as I waited for Trumaine to pick up. Try as I might, I had a hard time putting that dead-eyed kid together with Ira Lessing in Lessing's BMW. Len Trumaine had the same problem.

"It just doesn't make sense," he said after I'd told him most of what Finch told me. "Why would Ira give a ride to a punk like that?"

"Maybe he didn't have a choice," I said, playing devil's advocate. "Maybe he got jumped outside the car and was forced to drive off at knife point. You know that office of yours isn't in the best neighborhood."

"Yeah," Trumaine said, "but Ira knew that too. You saw the gate and the fence—it would have been a bitch for anybody to get in there at night."

"Lessing could've parked on the street."

"No way. Ira was compulsive. If he went back to the shop on the Fourth, he would have parked in the lot and gone in the side door."

"Well, if we rule out a mugging outside your building, that leaves only two possibilities."

"Which are?"

"That Lessing didn't go to his office on Sunday night, that he went somewhere else instead or in addition, and got mugged there."

"And the second possibility?"

"That he knew Carnova and gave him a ride."

"Knew him?" Trumaine said dubiously. "Knew him from where?"

I hadn't really thought it through, but Lessing's commitment to troubled street kids was one obvious answer. Carnova had a record of drug offenses. He might have passed through the Lighthouse Clinic. Or Kingston might have sent him to Ira for a handout.

I spun it out for Trumaine, at least as far as I could go. But Len didn't buy the idea.

"It's just not like Ira, Harry, to pick some kid up on a dark street in the middle of the night. I mean not unless the boy was in real trouble. Ira wasn't impulsive like that. He thought things through, you know? Planned them out. I'm not saying that he wasn't sincere about helping youngsters. He had a deep, genuine concern for disadvantaged kids. But he showed it in his own way—methodically, rationally, keeping everything under strict control. That's just how he was."

A philanthropist with the soul of an accountant. It was a weird combination.

"How did he get like that?" I asked Trumaine.

"Lord, I don't know. His dad, Tom Lessing, was a strict son-of-a-bitch. One of those dyed-in-the-wool Catholics who are really just Fundamentalists who genuflect. Ira didn't talk about Tom much, but I think he borrowed a lot of his behavior from him. And from Meg of course." Len sighed. "Maybe I'm wrong. Maybe he did give the Carnova kid a ride. Maybe he remembered the boy from Kingston's clinic. Or maybe Ira just stepped out of character for a minute. Christ, wouldn't that be awful?"

"Do you want me to nose around? Talk to Kingston?"

Len thought it over for a minute. "Let's discuss it

tomorrow morning—after I've talked with Meg and Janey."

"You're going to tell them all of it?"

"Hell, I don't know," he said miserably. "I don't know what I'm going to say. I mean, I don't know how I feel about it myself. It still doesn't seem real to me. It's like I'm playing a role I didn't try out for."

"I don't envy you."

Trumaine laughed. "That's all right, Harry. Nobody ever has."

9

. . . .

About seven the next morning the weather finally broke, with a sound like the roof caving in. A thunderclap shook me out of bed. A second one got me on my feet and moving toward the kitchen. I'd begun to brew a pot of coffee on my shiny new stove when the phone rang.

It was Len Trumaine. I could tell from his voice that something bad had happened.

"You think you could come over to the Lessings' house right away?"

"What's it about, Len?"

"The cops just called. They think they've found Ira."

"Alive?"

"Dead," Trumaine said in a numbed voice.

Even though I'd fully expected it, the news shocked me. "Do you know any of the details?"

"Not yet. The cops are on their way over right now —to fill us in. The family would like you to . . . well, to keep on top of things. Make sure we get all the facts. Try to find out how this could have happened."

"We may never know why it happened, Len," I said.

"We just want to be sure that every effort is made. That somebody . . . makes an effort."

"I'll do what I can," I told him.

The thunderstorm slowed traffic to a crawl on the interstate, so it took me the better part of an hour to make it to Riverside Drive. By the time I got there patrol cars were already lined up on either side of the narrow street—Covington, Newport, and Cincinnati police. The cruiser at the head of the drive was parked on an angle, blocking off entry. A Covington cop stood watch in front of it. The revolving flasher on top of his cruiser played against his wet slicker, turning it from bright yellow to a deracinated blue, then back to yellow again, as if the cop himself were some sort of weird warning sign placed beside a roadside accident.

"You're going to have to back on out of here," the cop said when I pulled up to him.

"I work for the Lessing family," I said. "My name is Stoner. Check me out."

"Wait a minute."

He walked over to the car, reached in, and pulled out a mike. As he talked into it I stared at the French Quarter house on the hill. The skeletal cane furniture on the terrace looked abandoned in the rain, like the bare bones of a deserted mansion. A moment later the cop came back.

"You can go in," he said. "But you'll have to park here."

I pulled over on the sidewalk beneath a dripping gas lamp and stepped out into the storm. By the time I made it to the terrace, I was soaked through. I knocked on the door, and Len answered.

He looked as if he hadn't slept at all. His eyes were bagged with fatigue. Beneath his too-tight clothes he smelled of nervous sweat and booze. Behind him the hall was filled with cops, all the way down to the living room.

"Christ, Harry, it's been an hour," Len said, giving me an exasperated look.

"I'm sorry, Len. The traffic held me up."

He glanced at the cops crowding the hall. In the gloom of the storm the Impressionist prints on the wall had lost all of their brilliance, like lights that had been switched off.

"His body was dumped on River Road," Len said, turning back to me. "In a field near the Anderson Ferry."

"How did the police find it?"

"An informer, I think. A girlfriend of Carnova's. Finch told me the name, but I forgot." He shook his head apologetically. "I'm pretty tired."

"Where is Finch?"

"In the living room, talking to Meg."

"And Janey?"

Len closed his eyes. "She's under sedation. It was very bad, Harry."

"Have they arrested Carnova?"

"Later today, I think. I missed some of it when Janey freaked out." His mouth started to tremble, and he clapped a hand across it. "Carnova tortured him, Harry. The little bastard tortured him. And then beat him to death and left his body to rot in the heat. Ira!"

Trumaine's face bunched up, and he began to cry.

I looked away. "I better talk to Finch."

"Yeah. Go." Len waved his free hand tragically. "Help Meg."

I made my way down the hall into the living room. Like the hallway, the room was crowded with cops and friends of the family. I recognized a few faces from the week before. I recognized the looks of the faces too.

Meg Lessing was sitting beside Finch on the white couch. She appeared to be in shock—her face flushed, her eyes fixed but unfocused. She held a rosary loosely in her hands. Finch glanced at me as I walked up to the couch. Meg Lessing followed his gaze as if she were under his spell.

The woman stared at me for a second, then frowned menacingly. "Why did this happen?" she asked. "Why have we been judged like this? Why couldn't He have shown mercy to a man who was so merciful?"

I looked down at my rain-soaked shoes.

"It's wrong." Meg Lessing turned to Finch. "All wrong," she said again.

"Mrs. Lessing," Finch said helplessly.

The woman folded her arms at her bosom and stared bitterly off into space, as if she couldn't be consoled. A Catholic priest with gray hair and a heavily lined face came over to the couch and sat down beside her. But she didn't see him.

Finch got up from the couch, looking shaken. Grabbing my sleeve, he pulled me out into the hall. Like Trumaine, he smelled of sweat and long, sleepless hours.

"God almighty," he said when we were out of the room. "You should have heard the wife! It was like Christ himself got nailed again."

"Lessing was a good man," I said softly. "They can't accept it."

Finch gave me an odd look. It wasn't contemptuous, but there wasn't any sympathy in it, either. I guessed he'd had his fill of wailing women and unanswerable questions.

"When did you find him?" I asked.

"About three this morning. The kid left the body under an old sheet of corrugated siding down by the Anderson Ferry. It's been lying there since a week ago

Sunday." Finch shuddered up and down his spine. "Lying there in all this heat."

"There's no question that it's Lessing?"

"Not in my mind."

"Trumaine said he'd been tortured."

Finch nodded slowly. "That's how it looks. We're still piecing the story together. We'll know better after we get the coroner's report and after we talk to the kid."

"You've got him?"

"We got him," Finch said. "Busted him on the Square about an hour ago. He'd been living in Fairmount with a girl named Kitty Guinn. She's the one who tipped us off on where to find Lessing's body and where to find Carnova."

"When are you going to interrogate him?"

"As soon as I'm done here."

"Mind if I tag along?"

Finch gave me another odd look. "Maybe you should," he said after a moment. "The press is bound to find out about this sooner or later. And the family should hear the whole thing before it comes out in the papers."

"Before what comes out in the papers?"

He glanced through the doorway into the living room, where Meg Lessing was still sitting, stony-faced, on the couch. "There are a couple complications you don't know about. You or the family. Things we found out when we busted Carnova."

"Like what?"

Finch ignored the question. "You coming with me?"

"Just give me a second to tell Trumaine."

He nodded and started down the hall to the front door.

10

. . . .

After telling Len I was leaving, I rode back across the river with Finch to the Justice Center, where Carnova was being held. I expected Art to explain himself on the way over. But it wasn't until we'd parked in the Justice Center lot that he began to talk. Outside, the storm banged and rattled like a drunk in an alley.

"We're going to treat this as a robbery-murder."

Finch said it with great deliberateness, as if it were a decision rather than a statement of fact.

"How else could you treat it?" I asked.

He pulled a cigarette from a pack in his shirt pocket and struck a match against the dashboard. "The arresting officers say that the kid claims he knew Lessing."

I'd thought of the possibility myself the night before. "Knew him from where?"

"That's the tough part," Finch said, breathing out a cloud of smoke. "From what we're piecing together, it looks like this kid, Carnova, was a hustler."

For a second it didn't sink in. "What kind of hustler?"

"He peddled his ass, Harry," Art said, looking aggravated with me for making him say it. "He's a homosexual prostitute."

I stared at him stupidly. "You're telling me that Ira Lessing was a homosexual who liked teenage boys?"

Finch sighed. "That's what the kid says."

"Carnova has to be lying."

"Maybe. We talked it over with the D.A.'s office, and

whether Carnova is bullshitting us or not, they don't
much like the idea of this coming up at the trial—the
fag angle. It might make a jury think twice, hearing
that Lessing had the hots for a teenager." He laughed
sarcastically. "I've got the feeling it won't sit too well
with the family, either."

"You've got that right," I said. I stared at him for a
moment. "You believe any of this?"

Finch stubbed the cigarette out in the dashboard
ashtray. "Let's just say it wouldn't completely surprise
me. Sometimes a family's the last to know when a rela-
tive goes south. I've seen it before."

I shook my head. "I don't believe it. This guy was a
straight arrow."

"Well, let's go talk to the little cocksucker." Finch
opened the car door and stepped out into the rain.

We went upstairs, to the fourth floor of the old
Court House. The main hall was filled with cops from
various jurisdictions, lounging against the walls, smoking, talking to each other. The place smelled like cops
—a stink of wet serge, muddy shoes, cigarettes, nervous sweat. I couldn't tell from the talk if any of the
cops had heard about the homosexual business. But
from the number of them standing around, I guessed
they knew something was up.

The interrogation rooms were located midway
down the hall. A group of beat cops stood outside one
of the paneled doors, laughing raucously. Finch
walked up to them and signaled to a tall sergeant. The
cop came over to him.

"He's inside?" Finch said.

The cop nodded.

"Is he talking?" Finch asked.

"Like it's a game show."

"Get us a stenographer, will you. Tell him to wait outside until I'm ready." The cop started off and Finch pulled him back by the sleeve. "Who's in there with him now?"

"Lennart and Tom Gerard."

"What about a PD?"

"He don't want one."

Finch gave the sergeant a look. "I don't want this queer to get off on some fucking Miranda shit."

"I'm telling you he refused counsel. Gerard read him his rights twice. The little bastard doesn't give a damn."

"What about the girlfriend?"

"We got her downstairs. You want her up here?"

Finch thought it over. "Yeah, bring her up with the stenographer."

The cop walked off. Finch glanced at me. "You know the routine, Stoner. Just keep out of the way. And keep your mouth shut."

Art walked over to the door of the interrogation room and opened it. Carnova was inside, sitting on one side of a rectangular table—his arms cuffed in front of him. Two sweaty shirt-sleeved cops were sitting opposite him. A pack of cigarettes and several Styrofoam cups of coffee sat on the table between them. There were cigarette butts all over the floor and clouds of stale smoke hanging loosely in the air.

Carnova looked up as Finch and I came into the room. He was short, shorter than I expected from the picture, and muscular in the arms and chest. He wore patched jeans, a studded belt, and a fur-lined leather vest open to the waist. No shirt, no shoes. Although his dirty angel's face was dry, you could tell that it had been wet with rain from the way the hair was plastered down on his forehead and cheeks. I took a good look at his darting blue eyes. I couldn't see any fear in them, certainly no remorse. Just the excitement of the moment, a kid's excitement at being the center of attention.

As he entered the room Finch took a Miranda card from his coat pocket and started to read the boy his rights. Before Art had finished Carnova was shaking his head and grinning.

"I ain't gonna get no lawyer," he said in a loud Appalachian kid's voice. "They just fuck you over, lawyers. That's something I learned from my dad."

Finch glanced at the other cops, then at the kid. "Okay." He pocketed the Miranda card. "You feel like talking about the murder, Terry?"

"I done it, and I'm ready to pay." The boy's eyes gleamed wildly. "Think I'll get the chair?"

"You might," Gerard said.

The kid lifted his chin dramatically, as if to say he could take it, and I suddenly realized that this was the biggest moment in his life—high drama. Like TV. Like *Perry Mason* or *People's Court*. It depressed me to think about the vicious, banal history that had led up to it.

"Unlock him," Finch said to Lennart.

The cop took off Carnova's handcuffs and snapped them on his own belt. Carnova rubbed his wrists.

"Thanks," he said to Finch, as if he'd done him a personal favor.

Finch grunted. "Don't mention it."

"I ain't gonna say nothing for the record, though," he said, with a cagey look on his face. "You got me fair and square. But I ain't gonna say nothing for the papers."

"Why, Terry?" Finch said.

"I got my reputation to think of." The kid reached out and pulled a cigarette from the pack on the table, screwing it in his mouth. "And I don't want my family to get involved."

"Family? You mean your girlfriend?" Finch said slyly.

"What about her?"

"She's already involved, Terry. She's right outside the door."

"Bullshit, she is. Kitty wouldn't come here. She's not that stupid."

One of the cops, Lennart, started to laugh. "She's the one who turned you in, Terry. She told us where to find you—and Lessing."

The kid gave Lennart an icy look. "You're lying. Kitty wouldn't turn on me."

"But she did, Terry," Finch said.

"Fuck you," the kid said. "I don't believe it."

Finch opened the door and waved to someone out in the hall. A moment later a skinny redheaded teenage girl with a pale, freckled face came to the door. She stared at Carnova for a second, and her lower lip began to tremble violently. The kid eyed her with astonishment.

"You done it to me, didn't you?" he said, as if he couldn't believe it. "You give me up."

"I done it for your own good," the girl said tragically, and started to cry.

"Oh, shit." The kid collapsed in his chair, the unlit cigarette dropping from his mouth to the floor.

"Wha'd you tell them, Kitty? Wha'd've you done to us?"

The girl let out a squeal of anguish, and Finch signaled someone to take her away. He closed the door again.

Carnova sat bent over for a long time, the very image of pained betrayal. But I had the feeling that, like all of his behavior, this was borrowed too—from some movie or TV show. The tough kid betrayed. After a time he looked up balefully.

"You can't believe everything that girl says. She ain't right in the head."

"She's right enough to hang you, Terry," Finch said coldly.

He ducked his chin again. "She told you all of it, did she?"

"She told us you killed Lessing, and she told us where you hid the body."

"No more'n that?" he said curiously.

"It's more than enough, Terry," Lennart said.

Finch said, "Your reputation's shot, son. And your girlfriend doesn't want you anymore. You ready to make a statement now?"

The kid sat in silence for a moment, his brow working furiously, as if he was sizing up his situation. "Why not? You might as well get the story straight, long as Kitty done opened her mouth."

11

. . . .

Once the stenographer came into the room, Carnova brightened up, as if he felt the spotlight on him once again.

Lennart and Finch sat down at the table. Gerard and I leaned against the walls.

"All right, Terry," Finch said. "Tell us about Lessing."

Carnova curled his lip in disgust. "He deserved killing—that faggot."

"I thought that's how you made your living," Lennart said. "Selling yourself to fags?"

Carnova looked deeply insulted. "It's just a gig, man. It's just a way of turning a dollar." He smiled a tough smile that made him look his age. "I ain't no fag myself. I hate 'em, man. I hate queers. I use 'em, that's all."

Gerard said, "You don't go down on them, Terry? You don't suck cock?"

"Hell, no! I let them go down on me. I make 'em pay to do it. Fucking fags."

"How about Lessing? Did he go down on you?"

"Sometimes," he said. "Yeah, sometimes I'd let him do me, if he paid good enough. But that really wasn't his bag, man. He liked . . . other things."

"How long have you known him, Terry?" Finch said.

"Since I was sixteen. We got together pretty regular since I was sixteen."

"How regular?"

"He'd cruise Monmouth in Covington 'bout once every two or three weeks, at the start. Last couple of years, I'd see him once a week over there, or over on Plum Street in Cincy down by Fourth. The johns have a signal worked out with the car lights. Everybody knows it. You flash four times, then turn off the lights if you're looking to catch. Five times if you're pitching. Ira'd come by, give the signal, and I'd hop in on the driver's side and drive us down by the river. He didn't want to go to any of the clubs. Only this year, sometimes, he'd go to the clubs."

"What clubs?"

"The Ramrod. The Underground. Like that." Carnova looked off into space. "He changed this year, some."

"How?"

"It ain't important," Carnova said, looking back at Finch.

"What about the night of the Fourth?"

"He picked me up on Plum Street. I got in the driver's side and he scooted over, like he usually did. He wanted to go to the riverfront, but I told him I needed some money."

"For what?"

"I wanted to cop some T's and B's. It was my birthday, and I wanted to get real high. So I said, 'Gimme your bread.' But all he had on him was a twenty-dollar bill. I said, 'Shit, you can do better than that.' And he says, 'I can give you a check.'" Carnova hooted with laughter. "I can't take no checks. So I drove down to the bank, there on Fifth, and I says, 'Gimme your damn bank card and I'll get some money.' And he says he don't have no bank card, when I know damn well

he does. So I smack him with the back of my hand."
He slashed the air with his hand. "I said, 'Gimme that
bank card.' But he won't. So I pull over and hit him
again. He starts crying and says now he don't use no
bank card. And I start waling on him . . ."

Carnova's voice died off.

"Why didn't he try to get away?" Lennart said.

"He was strapped in with the seat belt." He started
to say something else, then swallowed it.

Finch stared at him for a long moment. "You're lying about this, aren't you, Terry? About Lessing being
queer."

"No, I ain't lying," the kid said defiantly. "I'm telling you the truth."

Art slapped the kid—hard enough to knock him off
his chair. The other cops didn't move a muscle.
Carnova sat on the floor for a second, looking stunned.

"What'd you hit me for, man?" the kid said with the
true innocence of stupidity.

"I felt like it," Finch said between his teeth. "I may
feel like it again."

Carnova began to smile. "Sure. You wale on me as
much as you want. My old man used to wale on me.
See what it gets you."

He got to his feet, brushed off the seat of his pants,
and sat down again at the table. "See what it gets you,"
he said, giving Finch a fierce look.

Finch leaned back in his chair. "So you beat him up
because he wouldn't give you money."

"That's what I told you," Carnova said sullenly.

"According to the coroner, his skull was fractured
twenty-eight times, Terry. Six of his ribs were broken.
Both collarbones. The hyoid bone in his neck. His

right arm." Finch stared at the kid coldly. "Why'd you
do that, Terry?"

The kid ducked his head. "I don't know why," he
whispered.

Finch reached out and grabbed Carnova by his hair,
jerking his head up violently. "*You don't know why!*" he
shouted, looking directly into the kid's eyes.

The boy tried to pull away, but Finch had a good
grip. After a time the kid stopped struggling and sat
there, staring at Finch. A blush filled both of Carnova's
cheeks, and his eyes teared up with pain and indigna-
tion.

Finch gave the kid's head a good yank, then let go,
flinging his hand away as if it was contaminated. The
kid kept staring at him, tears running down both
cheeks, almost as if he was sorry for what he had done.

"I didn't mean for it to happen," he said angrily.
"He was good to me, most of the time. He gave me
things."

For a second I thought Finch was going to hit him
again. But Art held back.

"So you killed him for being good to you?" he said
dully.

"No, man!" Carnova said in an anguished voice. He
wiped the tears from his cheeks with both hands. "I
didn't mean to kill him. He just . . . he kept provok-
ing me. He wouldn't give me the money."

Carnova sobbed suddenly. It was startling, coming
from a kid like him—like hearing an animal make a
human sound.

"I drove from one bank to another, all over the fucking town," he said, beginning to cry in earnest. "I kept
giving him chances, man. But he wouldn't come

across. It was my birthday, man, and he wouldn't come across!"

Carnova sobbed again. "I was real high, from cele- brating. High on T's and B's. All I wanted was a few more dollars so's I could score again. I didn't want to come down, you know . . . I just wanted to stay up there for the whole day. But Lessing, man, he wouldn't give me the number."

"What number?"

"For the bank card, man. The password number. He just . . . wouldn't. So I got mad. I says to him, 'I'm going to show you, man. I ain't some little prick you can jerk around. I'm a man.' "

"What did he say?"

"He was kinda messed up. His face, I mean. He just kinda grinned at me like he was daring me on, you know. Like he didn't have no respect for me at all. Like he didn't care."

Carnova took a deep breath and wiped his face again. His nose was dripping snot and he wiped it, too, with the back of his hand. He sat there for a moment, breathing hard.

"I drove down to the Ferry, down there on River Road. And I pulled Ira out, and I says to him, 'I'm gonna give you one more chance.' But I can see he's pissed off now. I says, 'Give me the money.' That's when he hit me."

"Lessing hit you?"

"Yeah," Carnova said, as if he still couldn't believe it himself. "Ira shouldn't have done that, man. Not to me. Not that night. I picked up this rock and I hit him back with it. Right in the face." Carnova shuddered. "Man, it made a weird sound. Ira just kind of wobbled around and then he fell. I says, 'Get up!' But he ain't moving at all. That's when I start to get scared. I stoop down there and listen to his heart, and it's like . . . I couldn't believe it happened, man. He was dead. I started shouting at him, like, 'How can you be dead, man!' And then, I don't know . . . I just lost it. I started pounding on his face and his chest. Screaming at him, 'How come you're dead? You *can't* be dead!' Shit like that, you know. I mean I'm so pissed off that he's dead, I just can't think straight. I take this rock from the ground and start pounding his head with it, cursing him and crying and shit. I must've hit him a hunnert times. There's blood all over me."

Carnova's eyes lit up weirdly. "I tasted his blood, man. It was all over my face and my mouth, and I tasted his blood." The light in his eyes went out, and he slumped forward in his chair. "I drug his body over to this old shack. Put some siding over it. Drove around in his car for a few hours, then ditched it." Carnova looked up, exhaustedly. "That's about it." All four of us stared at the kid for a moment. Then Art stood up. "Did you get that?" he said to the stenographer.

The stenographer nodded.

"Good." Finch stretched his arms over his head, then slammed one hand down on the table in front of Terry Carnova, making the kid jump in his chair. "We're going to do this again, Terry. And again. Until we're satisfied with what we got. That okay with you?"

Carnova nodded stupidly, slumping back again in the chair. The defiant look he'd had on his face—that brazen, self-congratulatory look of celebrity—had vanished. He was just an ordinary kid now, who knew that his moment of glory had come and gone unapplauded.

Staring at him bent over in the chair, his dirty blond hair falling across his face like a veil, I tried my best to think of him as human. To think again of the ugly, predictable history that had made him what he was— the poverty, the ignorance, the abuse, whatever. I couldn't make myself do it. I couldn't make myself feel a thing for Terry Carnova.

When Finch started asking the same questions again, I got up and went out into the hall.

12

. . . .

Terry's teenage girlfriend, Kitty Guinn, was sitting on a bench outside the interrogation room smoking a cigarette. She stared at me pointedly as I walked by, holding up her right hand, like a kid in high school trying to get the teacher's attention. Greasy red hair braided in pigtails and fastened with bobby pins. A pale, freckled, red-eyed face, already aging, already old. No shape to speak of beneath a striped cotton shirt and jeans. I gave her a hard look, and she jerked her hand back quickly, ducking her head to her breast.

"Please, mister," she said in a nervous, down-home voice. "Are you a policeman?"

I shook my head, no.

"You ain't a policeman?" she said with surprise.

"My name is Stoner. I work for the Lessing family."

The girl dropped her eyes, as if the name Lessing meant something to her. "Maybe you help me anyways, Mr. Stoner? I just gotta talk to Terry."

"You're going to have to wait until they're done."

"When will that be, you think?" She looked up at a clock on the wall in front of her. "It's already 'bout four. And I got a bus to catch."

"It could take all night."

She thought about that for a second and made her face look grimly determined. "Then I just gotta wait. 'Cause I can't have him thinking what he thinks about me. And somebody 'round here's gotta hear me out." The girl gave me another pointed look.

It was obvious that she wanted to talk about Carnova. But I'd had my fill of her boyfriend, and the last thing I felt like doing was sitting there and listening to her apologize. On the other hand, I didn't want to blow the chance to learn more about Lessing. And judging by her reaction when I'd mentioned Ira's name, there was a possibility that the girl knew something worth listening to—something that Carnova hadn't admitted to or had distorted in his confession. Maybe it was a measure of how little I was looking forward to confronting the Lessing family with Carnova's story, but I decided to give the girl a chance to talk.

"I thought you turned Terry in," I said, sitting down beside her on the bench.

Kitty Guinn edged away from me self-consciously, just far enough to let me know that she wasn't the kind of girl who sat close to strangers. Under the circumstances it was a silly bit of redneck etiquette. But the fact that she had values of any kind gave her a big leg up on her boyfriend.

"I did turn him in," she said with a guilty look. "But I didn't expect it to happen like it done. It was Tommy T. that was behind it. Not Terry. I told the cops that when they come to get me. But they wouldn't listen."

"Terry didn't mention anybody else," I said to her.

The girl glanced disparagingly at the door of the interrogation room. "He's trying to make himself look big is all. 'Cause of what happened to that man."

"To Lessing?"

She bit her lip and nodded. "He was a good man, that man. He give Terry everything he wanted. When we didn't have no money, he give Terry money. He was good to Terry. And Terry . . . he liked him real good. Like he was his own dad that he never had."

"I thought Terry said he had a father."

"No, he don't. He don't have no one, save that old bitch aunt of his, over ta' Newport, and that bastard cousin of hers, Kent. Terry's own dad skipped out when Terry was a kid. And his mom . . . well, she married some guy up in Akron. Got her a brand-new family, and Terry ain't welcome. Terry didn't have nobody till he met me. Nobody but that man."

"Terry says that Lessing was a homosexual. That he paid him for his company."

The girl shifted her eyes away from me, as if she wasn't sure what to say. "I don't know nothing about that. He was good to Terry is all I know. There was never no trouble between them. And Terry ain't no fag, I can tell you that. He ain't never been no faggot. Them that says he is, like Chester Johnson and Tommy T., is liars." She looked at me again, proudly. "I *know* Terry ain't no faggot."

I believed that she thought she was telling the truth about Carnova's manhood. But then she didn't look like she'd had much experience with men. And she wasn't very bright.

"So you don't think Lessing was a homosexual?"

"No, I don't," she said stoutly, as if I'd talked her into it. "He was like a father to Terry. That's why he give him that money, 'cause he didn't have no kid of his own."

"Did you ever meet Lessing?"

"Once't, he come over to our apartment," she said shyly, as if the honor of it still sat heavily on her. "It was back in March. He bought us some pizza and

Terry played some music on his guitar. Terry's real musical." Her eyes shone with pride.

In spite of myself I'd begun to wonder why the hell she'd betrayed Carnova to the cops. Her love for the kid seemed genuine enough.

So I asked her, "Why'd you turn Terry in?"

Her face went pale with fright. "It was 'cause he got so crazy after it happened. He said he was going to hell. And it didn't matter no more what he done, 'cause he kilt the only person who ever did show him any kindness. He said he was gonna kill me too. Cut me up with his huntin' knife. And then he was gonna cut himself up." She put a hand to her mouth. "I got scared. That's why I called the cops. Terry kept talking about that body out there in the sun. He and Tommy T., they'd go and look at it 'bout every day. Like they was going to a ball game or something. Terry'd laugh about it with him. But when he'd come back, he'd act even crazier. The other night, he copped some T's and B's and got real high and took out that knife and held it to my throat, 'bout half the night. I kept tellin' him it weren't really his fault. That it was Tommy T. But that just made him madder. It was like half of him *wanted* it to be him that done it. And the other half jus' couldn't stand what he'd done."

She stared at me confusedly, as if Carnova's state of mind went way beyond her understanding. To be frank, it went beyond mine too. The tormented boy she was describing bore no resemblance to the vicious little bastard I'd seen in the interrogation room. It was a side of Carnova I didn't want to know about.

The girl must have read the revulsion in my face, because her own face grew hard-looking. "You believe what you want," she said stiffly. "But I done it to save him from himself."

The girl stopped talking to me after that. She didn't even want to look at me. She sat stock-still, concentrating on the door to the interrogation room as if her own fate were being decided inside.

I got up and walked down the hall to the CPD mess. Bought myself a cup of weak coffee from a dispensing machine. Sat down at a battered Formica table and stared out the corner window at the gray, turbulent sky.

I didn't know what to make of what the girl had said. She was desperate, and I had the gut feeling she'd say anything to make up for betraying Carnova to the cops. Some of her story had had the ring of truth—her terror was certainly real enough. But most of it was confused and confusing. Carnova's motivation for killing Lessing, the accomplice whom Kitty claimed had actually committed the murder, Carnova's crazy behavior after the crime. It was jumbled, I thought, because it didn't really make sense to her. Not any of it. Except for the fact that Lessing had been kind to Carnova. Like a father.

She hadn't actually accused Lessing of being a homosexual; but then she'd sensed that I didn't want to hear that, and she was sensible enough to play to her strength. If she knew that the homosexual charge might help Terry, she'd probably change her story to corroborate his. And a jury might buy the accusation.

I wondered if I did.

In spite of the fact that I didn't want to believe him, Terry Carnova made it damn easy to see Ira Lessing in terms of homosexual clichés. A harsh, puritanical fa-

ther. An icy, obdurate mother. A fragile, childlike
wife. A loyal, obsequious friend who did the real work
of holding things together. And a generous, good-
hearted, compulsively complicated man. A man whose
strengths and weaknesses I didn't pretend to understand.

Of course no one in the family, no one I'd spoken to
on the street, had given me the slightest reason to
think that Ira Lessing was gay. Only Carnova had
claimed that. A kid who made his living hustling
queers. A kid who was facing a death sentence and
looking for a way out, looking for a way to redeem his
manhood in front of the cops and in front of a jury.

As I sat there, mulling things over, Art Finch
walked into the room. He bought a cup of coffee and
brought it to the table.

"I'm taking a break," he said wearily.

"Has he changed his story?"

"He'll change it."

"Then you don't believe it? The homosexual crap?"

Finch took a sip of coffee. When he spoke he didn't
answer the question directly. "The fucking little queer
isn't going to squirm out of the chair on the basis of
some bullshit. Not if I can help it."

"The girlfriend claims he didn't do it. Or that he had
help."

Finch threw his hand at me disgustedly. "She'd say
anything now. You heard him in there. The kid admitted that he did it, and he didn't say a word about anybody else."

"What are you going to tell the family?"

Finch leaned back in his chair and sighed. "They're
downstairs right now. At least the mother and the guy

Trumaine are. That's why I'm taking a break. They're here to claim the body."

"Jesus."

"Jesus is right. Coroner says Lessing didn't have a face left."

I got up from the table. "I'd better go find them."

"Down in the morgue. Bottom floor."

"You coming?"

He nodded. "Eventually. I'm not in any hurry to do this. And I'd appreciate it if you'd pave the way."

"I'll do what I can." I stopped in the doorway and looked back at him. "Are you going to tell them about Carnova's confession?"

"Don't have a choice," Finch said. "Carnova'll have a PD by tomorrow. He'll *want* one after he gets done talking to the cons in the holding tank tonight. And even if he's too stubborn to listen to the jailhouse lawyers, the court's going to appoint a defender when he's arraigned. As soon as that happens some of this fag shit is going to make the papers. And it sure as hell's going to come out in court." He gave me a grimly determined look. "But there isn't going to be a word of it in the confession he signs. Not if it takes all night to get the truth out of him. You tell the family that."

13

. . . .

I found Len Trumaine and Meg Lessing in a tiny waiting room outside the morgue. A police matron was sitting with them, reading a magazine.

Trumaine tried to smile as I entered the room. But Meg Lessing didn't notice me. The woman was obviously in a bad way. Not just worn out, but worn away by the ordeal. Her handsome face looked seared by it, as if the flesh had boiled off, as if it were all hard white bone. It made her fierce eyes burn like candles in a skull. A coiled rosary sat on a table beside her, untouched.

I waved Len over to where I was standing in the doorway. In the fluorescent light his face looked green with fatigue.

"She shouldn't be here, Len," I said, glancing toward Mrs. Lessing.

"Don't you think I know that?" he said, giving me an exasperated look. "I tried to keep her from coming, believe me. But she started to make a scene. And that was something none of us needed." He glanced at the woman, sitting stock-still in the chair. "Meg has always prided herself on holding together in a crisis, on maintaining the family honor, no matter what. I've never been much on dignity myself. But it's her son, and she felt that one of the Lessings had to be here."

"She's not going to view the body?"

He shook his head violently. "Of course not. That's my job."

I patted his shoulder sympathetically. "How are you holding up?"

"I'm too worn out to say. If I had any personality left, I'd be dead drunk. Or hysterical, like Janey."

Behind us in the hall an orderly walked by, pushing a gurney loaded with a corpse. Len shuddered at the sound. "God almighty, what a nightmare."

I hated like hell to be the one to do it, but I was about to make things worse.

I took Len by the sleeve and edged far enough out into the hall so that Meg Lessing couldn't overhear us. At one end of the corridor a pair of steel doors led to the mortuary. Another loaded gurney was parked by the doors. A blue cloth lay across the corpse on top; one bare, bloodless foot protruded from underneath. Len stared at the body with horror.

It was a terrible moment to tell him about Carnova —I knew that. But I also knew that Art Finch would do it if I didn't, and I didn't want Len to hear the story from a cop. I didn't want the mother to hear it at all, not in the shape she was in.

"There's something you've got to know," I said. "Something about Carnova."

Len studied my face for a second, and I guess he could tell from my eyes that bad news was coming, because his own face fell. "Go ahead," he said in a sinking voice.

"The kid claims that he knew Ira, that he and Ira had a long-standing relationship."

"What kind of relationship?"

I stared at him sadly, not wanting to say it. "A homosexual one."

Trumaine gawked at me for a long moment. "You're joking."

"I wish I was. Carnova says that he and Lessing had been seeing one another for several years. He says that, on the night of the murder, Ira had picked him up for a sexual rendezvous. They had an argument over money, and the boy killed him."

"Over money?" Len said with a blank look.

"Carnova's a homosexual prostitute, Len."

At first Trumaine didn't react. Then his face got so red that he broke into a sweat, right there in that ice-cold mortuary hallway.

"That's the most outrageous fucking lie I've ever heard in my life!" he shouted.

"Take it easy, Len," I said, glancing nervously through the doorway at Mrs. Lessing.

But Trumaine didn't hear me. "First the bastard tortures Ira, then he murders him, then after he's dead he slanders him as viciously as you can slander another man!"

He'd gotten so worked up, I thought he was going to throw a punch at me.

"Why the hell did you tell me this, Harry?" he said, almost strangling on the words. "What did you expect me to say—that my best friend in the world was a queer?"

"No," I said.

"Then why tell me? Or did you figure I just couldn't make it through the rest of this day without hearing one more piece of vicious bullshit?"

"Len," I said, "I don't believe what Carnova said."

"But the cops do, right? I guess you can't be a kind, charitable human being—a decent man with a genuine concern for other people—without being labeled a queer."

"The cops don't believe Carnova, either," I said,

even though it wasn't strictly true. "They're going to pressure the kid into retracting the homosexual charge."

"Pressure him how?"

"What difference does it make?" I said, although it was going to make a difference to Carnova. "When the boy goes to court the D.A. will use his confession as evidence. And if Carnova or his lawyers try to introduce the homosexual crap, it won't be substantiated by the record."

"It won't be in the record?" Len said, starting to cool down.

"No. But that doesn't mean that it won't come out. Carnova's lawyers may feed the story to the press. And it's bound to get aired in court. I thought you should hear it from me first."

Len wiped the sweat from his eyes with his shirt sleeves. "I guess you're right," he said after a while. "I guess I had to know. I guess the family will have to know too."

"You still have some time. The papers probably won't get the story for a day or two. And they're bound to be skeptical in reporting it."

"Meg and Janey'll still have to be told." He sighed heavily. "Christ, it just keeps getting worse."

Finch showed up about five minutes after I'd finished telling Len about Carnova's confession. Together, the three of us went into the morgue to go through the formal process of claiming what was left of Ira Lessing.

It was a ghastly place. The cold steel examination tables, with the microphones drooping down above them like loose wires in an unfinished room. The freezer bank with too many doors. The dead-room stink of embalming fluid and disinfectant, and the faint sweet smell of flesh, like rot in a wall. The coroner pulled the body from the freezer bank. Something lumpy in a green zippered bag on a bright metal tray. Len stared at it for a long time—his face dazed.

"Are you sure this is Ira?" he said to the coroner.

The coroner nodded. "We've made a positive identification on the basis of dental records."

"Ira," Trumaine said again, staring at the body bag.

As we came back out into the lighted hall, Len broke down and sobbed. Finch looked away.

After a while Trumaine collected himself. "He'll go to the electric chair," he said, turning to Finch.

"You have my word on it," Finch told him.

I drove back to the Lessing house with Len and Meg Lessing. It had stopped raining by the time we got to Riverside Drive. Slanting sunlight broke through the storm clouds, drawing water from the hazy, distant hills. Already you could feel the fierce heat seeping back into what was left of the day.

I helped Meg Lessing out of the car and over to the stairs. She still didn't look as if she knew who I was.

I said, "I'm very sorry about your son, Mrs. Lessing."

"So am I," she whispered.

Gripping the handrail, Meg Lessing walked stiffly up the stairs. When she got to the top Don Geneva came out of the front door and helped her inside.

"I can't believe she's still on her feet," Len said, looking up at her.

"Is there anything else you want me to do, Len?"

"I can't think of anything—unless you could make

the whole thing go away." He stared at me for a moment, his face slack with exhaustion. "I guess we'll have to handle it on our own from here on."

I started to mention Carnova, then thought better of it. But the kid was on Len's mind, too, because he looked back at me as he started up the stairs.

"Ira was a good man, Harry. He really was. People won't forget that overnight."

"All right, Len."

I watched him walk up to the terrace, then I went over to the car and drove home.

14

Of course Lessing's murder made the front pages of both Cincinnati dailies and banner headlines in the northern Kentucky newspapers. The fact that Carnova was a male hustler was mentioned in each article, although no inferences were drawn about Lessing himself. In fact, the papers reported that Carnova had confessed to mugging Ira to get money to purchase drugs. Lessing was made out to be the random victim of a homicidal teenager.

It was obvious that Finch had succeeded in getting the boy to tell his story the way the D.A. wanted to hear it. When it came down to it, it was the way I wanted to hear it too. For the family, for Len. And for Lessing himself.

I hadn't known the man, but I'd met enough of his friends to form an opinion about him. And whether he'd been a closet homosexual or not—and I wasn't convinced that he had been—I figured he'd earned some slack from the media and from the rest of us.

Terry Carnova was arraigned on Tuesday morning and bound over to the grand jury without bail. An attorney was assigned to him by the court.

On Wednesday morning I went to the cemetery to see Lessing buried. It was a hot cloudy day, heavy with the promise of rain. A steady wind blew across the cemetery lawn, lifting the skirts of the canopy above the coffin and obscuring the voice of the priest as he spoke the final words. There were several hundred people at the graveside. I stood in the midst of the crowd, well away from the immediate family. When they lowered the coffin, Meg and Janey turned away, and Len Trumaine gathered them into his arms.

Because of the number of mourners, it took awhile for the traffic to clear out of the cemetery grounds. Rather than wait in the line of limos, I sat on a bench under an elm tree until most of the other cars had driven off. As I was sitting there Sam Kingston walked past me. At first I didn't recognize him without his doctor's white frock coat. Just another sad face in a sea of sad faces. But when I saw him stop by a car with the Lighthouse insignia on its door, I went over and said hello.

"Oh, hello," he said uncertainly.

"Stoner," I said. "The private detective who was working for the Lessing family? The guy who gave you the canceled checks?"

"Yes, of course," he said with a polite smile. "I couldn't place you for a second. I've had a tough time remembering anything this week."

"It's been a bad week, all right."

The smile on his face faded away. "It's a terrible loss. To the family. To the community. To me, personally. Honest to Christ, I haven't felt this bad since my father died."

"At least they got the kid who did it."

Kingston ducked his head, as if I'd somehow embarrassed him. "You know, we treated that bastard at the clinic."

"Carnova?"

"We treated him a few years ago. Nasty little redneck son-of-a-bitch. Loud-mouthed, selfish, ignorant and proud of it. The only reason he entered the pro-

gram was to get free methadone and to try to steal
drugs from the infirmary." Kingston stared at me balefully. "I keep wondering if that's where he heard about
Ira—from somebody at the clinic. Or maybe he saw
him there. Ira used to come in from time to time—to
say hello and talk to the kids. I don't know. It just
haunts me."

"You didn't make Carnova what he is, Doc."

"I know that," he said, straightening up. "It's just
. . . I'm going to miss Ira."

I stared across the access road at the deserted grave,
its canopy still fluttering in the hot wind. "He was
well liked."

"He was loved," Kingston said. "And when it comes
down to it, there really isn't anything better you can
say about a man."

Kingston started to get into the car, then turned
back to me. "By the way, I gave those checks you left
to a cop named Finch. He said you'd sent him to us."

"Yeah, I did."

"I got the feeling he didn't think they were important."

"They probably weren't. Did you ever show them to
your bookkeeper?"

He nodded. "Marty said a kid brought them in in
early June. I wasn't around, but Marty talked to him."

"It wasn't Carnova, was it?"

"No. I forgot his name. Just a teenage kid with a
handout." Kingston got into the car. "The sort of
thing Ira was always doing."

Several weeks went by, shot full of July heat. Between running credit checks and investigating insurance claims, I followed the progress of the Lessing case

in the newspapers. In early August, Carnova was bound over for trial, and a court date was set for the middle of September. About that time the papers began to hint at the possibility of a homosexual relationship between Lessing and Carnova, based on testimony at the grand jury hearings. The articles were buried in the local sections of the papers, perhaps out of deference to the dead man. But I couldn't help wondering how Janey and Meg had felt, seeing Ira smeared like that in print.

No one from the immediate family commented publicly on the accusation. All they could have done, anyway, was to deny it. And Meg Lessing was too proud a woman to dignify gossip about her son. But several of Lessing's friends, Don Geneva among them, called Carnova a liar.

As the days passed Geneva assumed the role of spokesman for the family, both in the papers and on TV. It was a tough job and it said something about the man—about his loyalty to the Lessings and to his dead friend—that he would volunteer so much of his time to insulate them from embarrassment and scandal.

I couldn't say exactly how I felt about seeing the thing finally come out in print. Outraged for Lessing and his family, certainly. But a little curious in spite of myself. About the grand jury hearings, about what would be said at the trial. On the whole, I guess, I was glad I was out of it—glad I'd never had to answer in my own mind the questions that were being raised about Ira Lessing's character.

Then, early in the morning on the first day of September, that all changed. Around 9 A.M. I got a call from Carnova's attorney, a guy named Jack O'Brien. He sounded polite and pleasant on the phone, but I found myself disliking him immediately. I knew why too—because he represented Carnova, because he was bent on dragging me back into the case.

All he wanted, he said, was a little of my time. Only I didn't want to give him that much of an opening.

"I've got a pretty busy schedule," I said brusquely.

"I can subpoena you," Jack O'Brien said in his affable voice. "In fact, I will subpoena you if I have to."

"For what? What the hell do I have to do with your client?"

"Let's not kid each other, Mr. Stoner. We both know that you witnessed Terry's confession."

It wasn't hard to figure out who'd told him I'd been in the interrogation room—the girlfriend, Kitty Guinn.

"Look, it'll only take a few minutes," O'Brien said. "Half hour tops. You'll save me some time and save yourself some grief."

O'Brien's office was in the Tri-City Building, on the corner of Fifth and Race, within easy walking distance of the Riorley. On the way over there I wondered what I was going to tell the guy. I already knew what he was going to ask.

Art Finch and the cops had worked hard on Carnova —to get him to retract the homosexual accusation, to get it off the record. It was a cinch that O'Brien knew that as well as I did.

Bullying the kid into changing his story, simply because the cops hadn't liked it, wasn't strictly legal. But in both versions of his confession Carnova had freely admitted murdering Lessing. And when it came down to it, that was all that mattered to me. Carnova was guilty, and I wasn't going to help him slip out of a death sentence. Even if I'd believed that the kid was telling the truth about Lessing's homosexuality, I'd have felt the same way.

So I made up my mind to lie to O'Brien if he questioned me about the interrogation. It wouldn't be much of a lie. Just enough to hang the little bastard.

15

. . . .

As law offices went, the Tri-City wasn't the high-rent district. O'Brien's suite was on the sixth floor at the end of a dark, dingy hallway, intermittently lit by greasy yellow fixtures and pale daylight filtering through the pebbled glass of office doors.

The furniture inside the anteroom was beaten at the legs and corners. The carpet smelled of mildew. The secretary, playing hunt and peck at the typewriter, looked like a temp. She buzzed O'Brien after I gave her my name, and he came out of an inner office to meet me. I guess I'd expected a younger man—an up-and-comer. But he was in his late forties. Thin, stoop-shouldered, bald. He had a movie mortician's face—long, dour, sunken, vaguely haunted about the eyes. He held out his hand and I shook with him.

"I just want you to know, before we start here, that I didn't take this case on my own. It was assigned to me by the court."

I nodded. "I understand."

"I don't like Terry Carnova. But he's my client, and he's getting a raw deal."

"He's getting what he deserves," I said.

"Why don't you hold off on that until I've had a chance to say my piece?"

He waved me through a door into the inner office. Kitty Guinn was sitting on a tufted couch across from O'Brien's desk. She didn't look at me as I sat down beside her. But I could tell from her pallid face that she was nervous.

O'Brien settled in behind the desk, shooing away some loose papers in front of him.

"You've met Kitty, I know." He smiled at the girl and she smiled back at him anxiously. She was wearing a white summer dress that made her look like a candle wrapped in tissue paper. "Kitty, why don't you tell Mr. Stoner what you've told me?"

"I done already told him," she said in a shaky voice. "Terry didn't kill that man."

O'Brien smiled without showing his teeth—tight-lipped, like a man with loose dentures.

"Is that it?" I said.

"That's part of it." He linked his fingers and settled his hands on the desk, leaning forward. "Terry Carnova is protecting a friend of his. A boy by the name of Thomas Chard. Tommy T. to his friends. It was Tommy who committed the murder. Terry's no more than an accessory."

"Bullshit."

"Yeah?" He leaned back again in his chair. "Let me ask you a question, Stoner. When Terry confessed to the murder, what weapon did he say he'd used?" He didn't wait for me to reply, which was a good thing because I had no intention of talking about the interrogation. "He said he used a rock, didn't he?"

I didn't answer him.

O'Brien smiled his toothless smile. "Well, let's just agree, for the sake of argument, that that's what he said. Anyway, it's on the record—one of the few things that is." O'Brien reached across his desk and fished out a piece of paper. "I have here a list of exhibits that the prosecution has prepared for disclosure. You want to look?"

"Why?"

"I thought you might notice that a couple of items are missing. Like a bloody tire iron found in the trunk of Lessing's car. Some jumper cables."

"So what?"

"I guess the prosecution didn't think they were evidentiary, huh?" He dropped the sheet of paper back on the desk. "Kind of hard to explain how Lessing's blood ended up on those items, if Terry just hit him with a rock."

"All you got for that is Carnova's word. He could have used any number of weapons."

"Then why isn't the prosecution presenting the stuff from the trunk as evidence?" He slapped his palm on the edge of his desk and Kitty Guinn jumped. "I'll tell you why. Because there's been a concerted effort to withhold certain facts in this case—facts that would make a murder-one conviction difficult or impossible to get. You know as well as I do that Lessing was a homosexual, that he'd been seeing Terry for better than three years, that on the night of the murder he'd picked Terry up outside a homosexual bar."

"I don't know anything like that," I said.

"Now who's bullshitting?" O'Brien said. "Let me tell you a few things you *really* don't know. For instance, I have a witness who will swear that Terry was driving Lessing's BMW on the afternoon of June 15, almost three weeks *before* the murder."

"And who would that be?" I said sarcastically. "His girlfriend here?"

Kitty Guinn stirred on the couch as if I'd prodded her with a stick.

O'Brien shook his head. "The guy's name is Quincey Calloway. He's the service manager at Riverbank BMW in Covington. He's prepared to testify that Terry brought the car in, waited for two hours while the car was serviced, and drove it off. Terry told Calloway that the car belonged to his father, and Calloway had no reason to doubt him until he saw the kid's photograph in the paper. Check it out if you don't believe me."

"So what? So Carnova was hired to run an errand. That doesn't prove anything. Lessing may not even have known about it."

"You don't really believe that, do you?"

"I believe that Carnova killed Lessing."

O'Brien shook his head again. "Christ, you people really want to crucify Terry, don't you? Why? Because he's a poor kid who made his living on the streets? Who learned how to fend for himself by watching guys like Lessing pick up eleven- and twelve-year-old boys on dark corners?"

"Save it for the jury," I said disgustedly.

"You'll be there to hear it, Stoner. I kid you not. Somebody in this case is going to have to start telling the truth about Ira Lessing."

"Whose truth? Carnova's? Kitty's here?"

"He didn't do it!" the girl exploded. "It was Tommy T. He kept egging him on, making like Terry weren't no real man, like he was soft for liking Mr. Lessing. Tommy T. was jealous is all. Pure mean and jealous, 'cause Mr. Lessing thought more of Terry than he did of him. That's how come it happened—pure mean jealousy. Tommy T.'s the one who started the hitting. He was showing Terry up. Showing him what Mr. Lessing was really like. Didn't Tommy T. tell Terry he'd done it to him? Didn't he tell him that very day that Mr. Lessing used to pick him up to have it done to him? He *liked* to have it done to him!"

I glanced at O'Brien. "To have what done to him? What the hell's she talking about?"

O'Brien didn't smile this time. "Look, I never met Ira Lessing. But the people I've talked to . . . well, they've told me he was a good man. A kind man. That's why I've held off on this for so long. I've kept it out of court and I've kept it out of the papers. But if you people don't stop lying about Terry's confession, you're not going to leave me a choice."

I was still confused. "Kept what out of the courts?"

O'Brien sighed. "Have you ever heard the phrase 'beat freak,' Stoner?"

I shook my head.

"It's street slang for a homosexual masochist. For a guy who likes to be hurt while he's having sex."

I laughed out loud. "You're telling me that Ira Lessing was a beat freak? That's quite a reach, even for a lawyer."

"You think I like it?" O'Brien said, flushing angrily. "I don't like any of this. But that happens to be the truth. Periodically, Ira Lessing hired Tom Chard to slap him, to punch him, to put his fist . . . inside him, to choke him almost to death while he masturbated."

O'Brien's face had turned bright red with embarrassment. "God knows how a man gets that way. I've talked to a forensic psychiatrist about it, and he says that some twisted part of Ira Lessing needed the punishment, the humiliation. He was irresistibly drawn to it, probably for most of his life. That part of Lessing was looking to be punished—for past sins, shortcomings, maybe for the masochistic need itself. Whatever the reason, he wanted to be badly hurt." O'Brien rubbed one of his red cheeks. "And I guess he got his wish."

I stared at him contemptuously. "So Lessing committed suicide? That's mighty damn convenient for your client. You're not actually going to feed that drivel to the papers, are you? That psychobabble?"

He didn't answer the question. "Ira Lessing didn't commit suicide. He was slowly and viciously beaten to death by Tommy Chard."

"What about Terry? What did he do, just sit around and watch?"

"Lessing's relationship with Carnova was different. Apparently, he was genuinely fond of the kid, and the kid thought of him as a father. It was Tom Chard that Lessing went to when he wanted . . . the rough trade. Tom Chard has the reputation for it. Ask about Chard on the street. Ask at the homosexual clubs—the Underground, the Ramrod. It was Chard that Lessing picked up on the night of the Fourth. Terry Carnova just went along for the ride."

I got up from the couch. "I don't believe a word of this crap. I'm not even sure I believe that Tom Chard exists. Hell, every prisoner in jail says he's the wrong guy."

"Terry Carnova didn't," O'Brien said coolly.

"And you know why?" I said, pointing a finger at him. "Because he's a fucking psychopath."

"Terry's a very screwed-up kid. But he didn't kill Lessing. Tom Chard did. And Terry confessed because . . . hell, I'm not even sure why myself. Because he didn't want to be a squealer. Because he wanted to be a big man. Because he looked up to Chard the way younger kids admire older brothers. Because he felt so guilty about what happened to Lessing that he thought he should be punished for it. Take your pick. And there's something else." O'Brien glanced at Kitty Guinn. "Terry was afraid for his family. For Kitty and his aunt. Afraid that Chard would do something to them if he ratted on him."

"You've got it all worked out, don't you?" I said. "The cops bust this kid, Chard. He and Carnova get separate trials. Each one makes a deal to cop out on the other. And neither of them gets the chair. The only guy that ends up dead is Lessing."

"Look, all I'm asking you to do is check out what I'm saying. Christ, you're a detective—ask a few questions. But I'm telling you now, if you and the cops and the Lessing family don't quit pretending that Ira was just an innocent victim, all of this is going to come out in court and in the papers. And you're going to be sworn in as a witness." O'Brien gave me a long, hard look. "I kid you not."

"What does the family have to do with it?" I asked him.

"She knows," the girl said, turning toward me with a wild look. "That man's wife knows. You ask her if she don't."

16

. . . .

The first thing I did, when I got back to the office, was call *my* lawyer, Laurel Gould. I didn't tell her about Carnova or Lessing. I didn't even tell her that I might be called as a hostile witness in a murder trial. Instead I asked her about Jack O'Brien—what kind of lawyer he was, what kind of man he was.

Laurel thought about it for a moment. "Uninspired about covers it."

"He's not a headline hunter? Or some sort of bleeding-heart ACLU type?"

"Just the opposite. He's a second-rate attorney with a conservative practice. He makes a living, but not a great one. I've never heard anybody say anything bad about him. But then nobody talks him up, either. I suppose he's competent. Why? Are you dissatisfied with the service at this window?"

"Christ, no. It's in reference to a case I'm working on."

"Meaning I'm not supposed to ask any more questions. Right?"

"Right."

She hung up.

I stared at the phone, thinking that I didn't want to hear what I'd just heard. I'd wanted Jack O'Brien to be a guy on the make, looking to get into politics, looking to get his name in print. The fact that he wasn't didn't make me believe what he'd said. There were just as many sincere idiots as there were insincere ones. But it sure as hell made him harder to dismiss.

Just so I could tell myself I'd done the right thing, I picked up the phone again and called Art Finch at the CPD.

"Long time no hear," he said, as if he wouldn't have minded if it had been longer still.

"I just got done talking to Jack O'Brien."

"Yeah?"

"He's threatening to make a stink if you guys don't release Carnova without a trial."

Finch laughed.

"Seriously," I said. "O'Brien claims he's got some nasty information about Lessing that he's going to give to the press."

"I know all about it," Finch said. "He came to us, too, last month."

"Then you don't believe him?"

"Hell, no. All he's got is Kitty Guinn's hearsay. And she's in the bag all the way. The girl's a junkie, in case you didn't know. Jack probably didn't mention that, did he?"

"No, he didn't."

"Sure, we heard that shit about Lessing's love life. And we heard about the so-called real killer. What the hell did you expect him to come up with? He's got no defense at all unless he can discredit Lessing. Or unless we've got the wrong boy."

"You don't, do you, Art?"

Finch's voice hardened in a hurry. "You're not about to go south on us, are you, Harry?"

"I'd just like to make sure that the guy I'm helping you convict is the right man."

"You know fucking well he's the right man. Jesus

Christ, you heard the scumbag confess. Do the world a favor and save your sympathy for Lessing."

"What about Tom Chard?"

"What about him? He's a bad boy. But there's no one but the girl to connect him to Lessing. Besides, he's got an iron-clad alibi for the night of the Fourth. He spent the evening with some fag named Coates."

"You checked it out?"

"Yeah," he said disgustedly. "We checked it out. And if you don't mind, I got better things to do than hold your hand."

"One last question?"

"What?"

"Why aren't you using the items from Lessing's trunk as evidence? The tire iron and cables?"

"Jeez, even you should be able to figure that out. We didn't get any usable prints off the stuff. No prints. Got it?"

"So you can't tie them directly to Carnova."

Finch grunted. "Right. Now, are you satisfied? Or do you want I should arrange a home visit from Terry?"

I let it go after that. If I got subpoenaed . . . well, I'd worry about that when it happened, although I think I already knew I'd lie on the stand. I toyed with the idea of phoning the Lessings or their spokesman, Geneva, to let them know about O'Brien's threat. But I was weary of bringing bad tidings to that bedeviled family. Besides, there wasn't anything they could do to change things. Either Kitty Guinn's story would come out or it wouldn't. What the Lessings did didn't matter.

That was a Tuesday. Two days later, on a Thursday

afternoon, Terry Carnova's aunt showed up in my office.

Of course I didn't know it was his aunt until she'd introduced herself. At first sight I thought she might be a hooker. She was short and well built. Maybe thirty years old, with a tough, handsome, experienced-looking face, heavily made up around the eyes and mouth. Her short copper hair was set in curls, little ringlets that danced along her forehead and down either cheek like wire springs. She wore tight-fitting jeans and a white cotton blouse tied in a knot beneath her breasts.

There was a teenage boy trailing after her. A thin, sullen-looking kid, with a burned-out face that reminded me of Kitty Guinn's—parchment-white and old beyond its years. He wore his bleached blond hair in a Mohawk, dyed purple at the tips and growing out mud-brown at the roots, like a two-tone Chevy with a pinstripe.

"You Stoner?" the woman said in a down-home voice.

I said, "Yes."

She had a cigarette in her mouth, and the smoke crawling up her face made her wince. "I'm Naomi Trimble—Terry Carnova's aunt. And this here is Kent Holliday."

The boy nodded perfunctorily.

"What can I do for you, Ms. Trimble?"

"Don't know if you can do anything."

She took the cigarette out of her mouth, cupped her hand, and tapped the spent ash into her palm.

"There's a tray right there," I said, pointing to the corner of the desk.

The woman walked over and stubbed the cigarette out, brushing the ashes from her palm.

"I ain't never been in a detective's office," she said. "I ain't never had no trouble I couldn't handle on my own—up till now. But I guess I got to talk to somebody, or Kent here does."

She glanced at the teenage boy, who was still staring sullenly around the room.

"Look," I said. "I'm not the guy you want to talk to. I don't have anything to do with Terry's case."

"You got something to do with it," the woman said with certainty. "I heard Kitty say your name and how you was going to testify for Terry."

"Kitty's dreaming. If you've got something to report, talk to Jack O'Brien, Terry's lawyer."

"I ain't gonna talk to no lawyer," the teenage boy said, with such ferocity that I turned in the chair and stared at him.

"Why?"

He stared back at me defiantly. " 'Cause I ain't gonna testify in no courtroom is why. I ain't gonna do that bitch Kitty Guinn no favors neither. Not the way she bad-mouths me and Naomi."

The woman gave the kid a long-suffering look. "Hush up with that stuff now. That ain't what we come to talk about."

Turning to me, she said, "It's true that girl and me don't get along so good. I just ain't that fond of junkies, always sneaking around and stealing stuff. And as far as going to Terry's lawyer, well, he ain't interested in talking to us neither."

"How is that?" I asked.

"To tell you the truth, he come by about a month ago looking for me to be a, whad'ya call it, character witness. Only I didn't have nothing good to say about Terry, so he left all pissed off. Pissed off Kitty so damn much that she threatened to shoot me." The woman shook her head stubbornly. "But I ain't gonna be intimidated by no threats. I told him and I'll tell you, Terry's been a burden to me since he was twelve years old. Always in trouble, always on the street. I tried to do the best I could by him, but the fact is, I ain't cut out to be nobody's mom."

She touched the tight knot in the shirt beneath her breasts as if she were touching her heart. "I work nights and sleep most of the day. Ain't much of a cook and ain't much on cleaning house. The little time I have to myself, I don't want to spend keeping an eye on some wild kid. I told Estelle that when she brought Terry by six years ago. But there wasn't really any other family to leave him with—what with his daddy run off and Estelle having her problems with the booze. So I let her talk me into looking after him till she got back on her feet. Then she went off and got married to some guy who didn't want to hear about no other children, and I got stuck with Terry. First night I had him, he run over to Fourth Street with some of those boys. Didn't come back till Friday, stoned out of his head and smelling like a brewery. Been that way ever since. Soon as I leave the house he just runs off and ends up in trouble. Used to be I could whup him or scare him with the truant officer. But since he got so damn big and mean, I've been afraid to do anything. And once he got tight with that Tommy T., well, I could see the handwriting on the wall. I just knew Terry'd end up killing somebody, and, by God, he did."

I was surprised by her candor. And even more surprised by the fact she wasn't defending Carnova. "You knew how he was making his living?"

The woman ducked her head. "Yeah, I knew. I never come right out and said it to myself. But I knew he was shaking queers down to get money to cop T's and B's. Him and Tommy T."

"What do you know about Ira Lessing?" I asked curiously.

"Not a thing," she said flatly. "Never heard his name before I read it in the newspaper. Kitty says that he and Terry were real close. But I never saw it. Course for the last couple of years, Terry's been living over on Baltimore with Kitty, so I ain't seen that much of him. Could be Terry and him were close. But I doubt it."

"Why?"

"Well, for one thing, Kitty'd say about anything to help Terry out after she turned him in. And for another . . . Terry just don't have no feeling in him. I mean not so's he'd be friends with a man like that Lessing. The way Terry grew up, he lost all his respect for other people. Not having a daddy. Bouncing around from place to place, with Estelle getting so drunk she'd have to be locked up, and Terry getting farmed out while she dried out. That just killed all his sympathy."

She ducked her head. "Maybe I didn't help any neither. I ain't fit to be nobody's mother—I know that. But I do believe Terry was far gone before he ever met me. He was headed down that road anyway. And he finally got to the end of it. Least that's the way I was thinking till I talked to Kent last night. Now I ain't so sure."

"Sure of what?"

"That Terry kilt that man."

Naomi Trimble was a hard, loveless woman living in a hard, loveless world. She had a great deal to pay back for, but self-delusion didn't seem to be one of her sins. She wasn't being dishonest about herself. And I had the feeling that she wasn't being dishonest about Terry Carnova.

I glanced at the boy—Kent Holliday. He tilted his head and stared down his nose at me, contemptuously. A tough street kid, not about to give an inch to an adult. I knew Carnova wasn't any of my business—not anymore. But part of me was damn curious about what it was that had changed Naomi Trimble's mind. I let that part win out.

"What do you have to say?" I said to Kent.

"I know what happened to that man," he said in a sullen voice.

"Lessing?"

He nodded slightly.

"You were there when he was killed?"

"After. They picked me up in that car after, over to Elberon."

"What car?"

"BMW. It was real messed up inside. Terry said it was on account of they had a fight with a nigger. He said his dad was gonna be real pissed off 'cause it was his dad's car and they done ruined the seats."

"I thought Terry didn't have a father."

"He don't," Kent Holliday said. "That's just what he called this guy who give him money and clothes and shit. This guy Lessing."

"You saw him with Lessing?" I said.

"No, I never did. But somebody sure as hell give Terry a lot of money pretty regular. And I saw Terry driving that car a couple times before—only he was always alone before."

"Who else was in the car that night?"

The boy hesitated a second, and Naomi Trimble gave him an angry look.

"Go on and tell him."

"It was Tommy T.," Kent said.

I stared at the boy's face. He was still trying to look tough, but it had cost him some brass to say that name. "You're afraid of Tommy T.?"

The kid laughed a scoffing laugh. "Hell, yes, I'm scared of him. Anybody got any sense at all is scared of Tommy T. He's a bad-ass dude."

"Is that why you don't want to go to court?"

Kent nodded. "He knew I was talking to you now, he'd come looking."

"Then why are you here?"

The boy glanced at the woman. " 'Cause of her," he said. "She's my second cousin."

It was like the flip side of Len Trumaine and Janey Lessing—the down-home version.

"Tell him what happened, Kent," Naomi Trimble prompted.

The boy looked at me and I said, "Go ahead."

He took a breath. "Soon as I got in the car, I could see Tommy T. was real high. He's snapping his fingers. And stamping his feet. And singing to the music on the radio. Every once in a while he starts laughing like crazy. Terry starts singing and laughing, too, like it was all some big joke. Only I can tell he ain't really into it the way T.T. is. He's just copying him, like he always does. We head on down Ninth, playing that radio s'loud as she'll go. T.T. says to Terry, 'That was some good show.' Talking about the fight, you know?

And Terry says, 'Yeah.' And they both laugh some more. Then T.T. says, 'Let's go on over to Coates's so's I can get me some new clothes.' 'Cause he's got blood up and down his shirt and pants from the fight. So Terry goes on down to Walnut Street and parks in front of the Deco. And we go up to Coates's place."

"Who's Coates?"

"He's this fat old faggot lives in the Deco apartment house, across from the Ramrod. He's got the hots for Tommy T. Do 'bout anything for him. Man, Tommy treats him like shit too." The boy laughed as if it was funny.

"Anyway, we get on upstairs and Coates lets us in. Tommy T. says to him, 'Give me some fresh clothes, you old faggot.' Then T.T. takes off his shirt and pants in front of him. Coates, he gets all hot and bothered and asks Tommy if he'll do him right there. Tommy grins and says, 'I will if you pay me fifty dollars. You gotta wash out my old clothes and ream my asshole too.' Coates says he'll do anything for some of that. So they go on back to the bedroom and—"

"I get the picture," I said sharply.

The kid looked shocked. It wasn't embarrassment. Judging from the way he'd been talking, there wasn't much that could embarrass him. It was the fact that he'd embarrassed me. It made his face turn red and his eyes go cold, brought his redneck pride to life—that fierce sense of propriety that had sent Kitty Guinn squirming away from me on the CPD bench. I'd inadvertently underlined the distance between his world and mine, and he didn't like it.

"Go on now," Naomi Trimble said gently, as if she were trying to soothe his sense of injury.

But it took a few moments for him to start up again,

and, at that, I could still hear the wounded pride in his voice. "Me and Terry stayed in the living room while T.T. and Coates was . . . doing their thing." The boy gave me a withering look. "Soon as Coates and T.T. left, Terry starts acting crazy. He walks up and down in front of the couch, talking to himself and cussing. Then he starts tearing up the place. Pulling open all them drawers and closets. He says to me, 'Kent, I need to find me some more T's and B's right now. I need to stay high. It's my birthday today. And I'm gonna party the whole night long.' Then he says something that jus' knocks me out. He says, 'You know my dad give me that car for my birthday. He give it to me 'cause he's going away.' Man, I could not believe it!"

The kid looked off into space, as if he were still tasting the beauty of it. I heard the woman say, "Go ahead."

"Well, we's sitting there for a time, then we start hearing Coates in the other room, screaming and crying. That just seemed to freak Terry out more. It freaked me out some too. He jumps up and says. 'Fuck it. I ain't staying here.' He goes on over to the door, then he stops and takes them car keys out of his hip pocket and just drops them on the floor. He says, 'You tell Tommy T. he can have that car.' And I say, 'What're you doing, man? Your dad give you that car!' And he says, 'No, he didn't. He didn't give me nothing.' He looks at me real hard and he says, 'Kent, Tommy and me kilt a man tonight. And that's how come we got that car.' Then he walks out the door. Man, I lit out of there too. I wasn't gonna stick around after hearing that."

I glanced at the kid. His eyes were as stunned-looking as they must have been when he'd heard Carnova confess.

"I thought it was the drugs talking," Kent said. "I swear to God I did. But just the same I didn't go near Terry nor Tommy T. for a couple days. Then on Sunday, me and my partner, Jamey, was walking down by the Terminal, and we saw that car sitting there with all them cops 'round it. And I knew it had to be so." He shook his head sadly. "Just had to be."

"So you called the police?"

"No, I never. But Jamey . . . well, I told him about it, and he went on down to a pay phone at the Hi-Lo and called it in. Jamey's father's a preacher, and then he never liked Terry none, anyway."

"Why didn't Jamey tell the cops about Tommy T.?"

Kent ducked his head. "Scared of him, I reckon."

I glanced at the clock on my desk and thought of Len Trumaine looking up at the big iron clock on the Union Terminal facade. It was 4 P.M.

"Where could I find Tommy T.?" I asked the kid.

"Sometimes he's over to the Underground on Fourth. Sometimes he's down there at the Ramrod on Walnut. That is, if he ain't with no john."

"You gonna look into it, then?" Naomi Trimble asked.

I stared at her a moment and said, "I'll think about it."

17

· · · · · · · · · · · · · · · · · · · ·

Before Naomi Trimble left I asked her outright if she believed Kent Holliday's story. The boy snorted with outrage, but the woman understood where I was coming from.

"I guess I must," she said, "or I wouldn't be here."

She gave me a thoughtful look. "I didn't want to believe it, no more'n you do. Terry's a bad seed. I know it and I know he's gonna stay that way as long as he lives. He coulda kilt somebody easy. In fact, I was sure he did till I talked to Kent. But when you add what Kent says to the story that girl, Kitty, tells . . . well, I guess there's room to doubt. And I can't make myself think it's right Terry should die without somebody finding out for absolute sure. I'll tell you something else, too, something I've been thinking on. That man Lessing, he wasn't a god like the newspapers make him out. He couldn'a been. I ain't saying he was Terry's sugar daddy, like Kitty claims. I can't believe he was. But I do believe there must've been something 'tween him and Terry. Or how else do you explain it?"

She shrugged as if the answer was beyond her, as if it was enough that she'd posed the question. She took Kent by the arm and walked out, leaving the finding of answers to me.

For a few seconds I just stared at the desk, wondering why I'd put myself back in the case. It would have been easy enough to dismiss Naomi and the boy before they'd had a chance to tell their stories. But I hadn't done that. Even though they'd come to me by mistake, I hadn't done that. And now it wasn't easy anymore.

It wasn't that I felt sympathy for Carnova. I didn't. I knew as well as Naomi Trimble did that Terry was guilty enough—whether he actually did the murder or not. Only there was a difference between guilty enough and guilty before the law. The woman had faced that fact. Now it was my turn.

What if Carnova *had* been an accomplice? I asked myself. He was still an accessory to murder. Finding the truth of it wouldn't change that. It wouldn't change the terrible thing that had befallen Ira Lessing, either. What if I let it slide?

I stared at the desk again. The woman had written down her address on State Street in lower Price Hill and left the tag of paper on my blotter. She didn't leave a phone number—presumably, she didn't have a phone.

I picked up the slip with her address and stuck it in my pocket. Then I picked up the phone and called my friend George DeVries, an investigator at the D.A.'s office.

"I need a favor, George," I said.

"Like what?"

"Run a name through CID for me. Tom Chard, a.k.a. Tommy T. He's a West End juvie. See if you can dig up a mug shot and an address."

"An address won't mean much for a kid like that."

"See if you can get one anyway. I'll come by in about an hour or so with an envelope with your name on it."

He laughed. "Just make sure there's a President's name inside."

* * *

Once I'd finished with George I took the elevator to
the street and walked downtown to Jack O'Brien's office. I hadn't decided what I was going to say to him
even as I knocked on the door of his run-down suite.
As it turned out, he didn't give me the chance to make
up my mind.

As soon as the secretary ushered me into his office,
O'Brien's mortician's face got red, from his sunken
cheeks to the top of his bald head. He'd been reading a
brief—half-frame glasses on his nose, feet up on the
desk. When he saw me come in, he dropped his legs to
the floor and sat bolt upright in his chair.

"What the hell do you want?" he snapped.

"To talk about the Lessing case."

O'Brien laughed bitterly. "Tell the Lessings to send
another boy."

"I don't work for the Lessings anymore."

"Sure, you don't." He pulled the half-frames from
his nose and tossed them on the desk. "Listen, Stoner,
everybody works for the Lessings. The cops. The D.A.
The papers. In fact, some fat guy named Trumaine
came by my office the day after I talked to you and
tried to hire me too. Funny about the timing, huh?"

"Len tried to bribe you?" I said with surprise.

"In so many words. Mostly he rattled on about what
a great guy Lessing had been and how much the family
had already suffered and how none of their friends
wanted to see them suffer anymore. The message was
clear. If I kept the homosexual stuff out of court and
out of the the papers, Ira's friend would be 'grateful.'"

I stared at him hard. "I didn't tell the family what
you told me about Carnova—or about Chard."

O'Brien gave me a thoughtful look, then picked up

the glasses and began spinning them around by the earpiece. "Well, somebody must have told them some of it —enough to get them upset. What's more, somebody's been talking to Kitty Guinn."

"Meaning?"

"Meaning she's been receiving threatening phone calls almost hourly, and she's scared. Hell, it's worse than that—she's almost crazy, ranting about enemies and settling old scores and, at the same time, so frightened she shoots up three or four times a day. It's a miracle she can function. We've got the preliminaries coming up next week. If she goes over the edge, I might as well plead the son-of-a-bitch guilty as charged. That's probably what it'll come down to anyway, even if Kitty does testify. I'd try to plea-bargain if I had anything solid to bargain with."

"Won't Carnova testify in his own behalf?"

"You know better than to ask that," O'Brien said flatly.

But I had the feeling that he wasn't about to put Terry Carnova on the stand. As far as I knew, Carnova had never recanted his confession. Which meant that O'Brien's defense rested exclusively on extenuating circumstances, on Kitty Guinn's testimony about Chard. At least it did at that moment.

I stared at O'Brien for a second, at his dour face. "Hold off on any plea bargaining for a while."

"Why? So you can make damn sure everyone else's nailed down?"

"Just hold off," I said evenly. "Give me a chance to look into a few things."

O'Brien curled his lips sarcastically. "Don't tell me. You've had a change of heart."

"I talked to Naomi Trimble this afternoon."

"That's great. Just great. The woman is as bad as the Lessings. As far as she's concerned, the kid's as guilty as sin. Never mind that she helped to make him what he is. Never mind that her holier-than-thou attitude doesn't extend to her own life and character, which are about as low as you can get."

"She's changed her mind," I said. "She thinks Terry didn't do it now. She thinks Tom Chard did. And she's found a witness who can confirm some of Kitty's story."

O'Brien stopped twirling the glasses and stared at me, slack-jawed. "Why didn't she come to me?"

"Because the witness is a kid who doesn't want to testify in open court."

O'Brien's jaws snapped shut, as if he had Kent Holliday between his teeth. He leaned forward, hooking the glasses around his ears and staring at me belligerently. "I'll subpoena the little bastard. Just tell me his name."

"Take it easy with the subpoenas, okay? They won't do any more good with the kid than they would with me."

"Then what do you suggest I do?"

"I told you. Sit tight. Let me poke around. Nobody wants to see Lessing's killer go free."

"I wish I believed that." He leaned back again and squinted at me down his nose. "Does this mean you'll testify about the doctored confession?"

I shook my head. "I'm making no guarantees about that."

"Then what are you guaranteeing?"

"That I'll look into Kitty's story," I said.

"And what if you don't come up with anything?"

"Then you're out a couple of days. And Carnova's no worse off than he is now."

'No better, either."

"It's the best I can do," I told him.

I caught a cab outside the Tri-City Building and took it up to Government Square. I could have walked the six blocks easily, but it was getting late, and it was hot, and I wanted to catch George DeVries before he left for the day.

I just did catch him, stepping out the door of his office on the second floor of the Court House. A tall, paunchy, red-haired man, with a face so netted with wrinkles that it looked like something drawn on crumpled butcher's paper. I'd known him for fifteen years, and in all that time he'd never done me a favor without a payoff.

"Thought you were going to stand me up," George said with his wrinkled grin.

He reopened the office door and waved me through.

"Did you get it?" I asked him.

He handed me a folder from off his desk. "Right in here. Mug shot. Rap sheet. The works. Now how about the envelope?"

I pulled a twenty from my wallet. "Buy your own stationery."

He stuck the bill in his shirt pocket. "Anything else I can do for you?"

"You can tell me what's new with the Lessing case."

"Yeah, I heard you were on that. Art Finch told me."

"I'm just a bystander, George."

"Well, bystander, you don't have to worry about a conviction. We got this kid cold, and you can tell the family that."

"You're the second guy this afternoon who thought I was still working for the family."

"You're not?" George said with surprise.

"Not anymore."

"They've been sending so many people through this office, I figured you were part of the crowd."

"They've been conferring with the D.A.?"

"That's one way of putting it. What they're doing is pressuring him, politely but persistently. They want that kid convicted. And they want the conviction *clean*. No extenuating circumstances. No more nasty headlines. If you get my drift." George stared at me with naked curiosity. "This guy Lessing . . . I've been hearing a lot of rumors about him over the last few weeks. Maybe some of it's true?"

"I don't know, George. I never met the man." I glanced at the folder in my hands. "Chard's name hasn't come up in the Lessing investigation, has it?"

He shook his head. "Haven't heard him mentioned. Just Carnova. He's the whole ball of wax as far as I know. Why? Is Chard a witness or something?"

"Could be, George," I said, slipping the folder under my arm and heading for the door.

Or something.

18

. . . .

I walked back to the Riorley Building from the Court House through the sultry September twilight. Upstairs in my office, I flipped on the desk lamp and spread the contents of George's folder on the desk in front of me.

At first look I could have mistaken the rap sheet for Terry Carnova's. It detailed the same history of petty crime, the same progression from B and E's to possession to assault. But as I scanned the charges I noticed that Tommy T. also had several aggravated batteries on his record and a rape. Even though the felonies had been dropped, it made Chard look, on paper at least, a little nastier than his pal Terry, a little more openly prone to physical violence.

The small amount of personal history on Chard's rap sheet suggested a miserable childhood. There was no listing for a father. His mother had died at the age of twenty-three. Chard had spent several years in an orphanage, graduating to reformatories when he was twelve. His formal schooling stopped at the fifth grade. He had no record of employment. He admitted to drug and alcohol dependency, for which he'd been treated twice. The rap sheet didn't indicate where he'd been treated. But it would have been interesting if it had been at the Lighthouse Clinic—on Ira Lessing's money.

Whether he was connected to Lessing or not, Chard was virtually the same kid as Terry Carnova, a couple

of years older, a couple of inches taller, a little more
hardened to the ways of his world. He even looked a
little like Carnova in the mug shot. Curly blond hair,
cupid's mouth, a sordid kind of handsomeness. But
where Terry had seemed a demonic altar boy, this one
had no boy left in him at all. His wide eyes and pale
irises gave him the nervously alert, deadly stare of a
big cat on the prowl.

Chard had last been arrested, for battery, three
months before, in late May. The address he had given
at the time was in Price Hill, on Grand Street. I wrote
it down in my notebook. Then I pulled the directory
out of the desk and looked up the two clubs Tommy T.
was known to frequent. I didn't think about why I was
doing it. I just did it.

The Underground was located on Fourth Street, between Plum and Central. The Ramrod was located on
Walnut between Sixth and Seventh. I couldn't find a
listing on Walnut for anyone named Coates, but Kent
Holliday had said that the Deco Apartments were
right across the street from the Ramrod.

I put the phone book back in the desk drawer,
clicked off the lamp, and sat there awhile longer,
watching the twilight fall through the office window.
Then I went out.

It took me about ten minutes to drive across town,
over the Ninth Street viaduct, into lower Price Hill.
One look at the street traffic—heavy on that hot Thursday night—and you knew it was an Appalachian
ghetto. The people all had the same fierce, wan,
burned-out faces—faces marked in equal measure by
grinding poverty and an unquenchable redneck pride.

Boys walked by with beer cans in their back pockets,

cigarettes aslant in their mouths, suspenders flapping, unhitched, at the sides of their jeans. Teenage girls— their shorts tight across their bellies, their tube tops rolled at the breast—shouted obscenities at passing cars, then scattered amid wild laughter when the drivers slowed down to stare. Men in grimy work clothes trudged home from bus stops while their women sat on the sidewalks in folding lawn chairs, staring at TV's propped on casements and front stoops.

Above State, where the hill began, the pedestrian traffic thinned out. Little streets veered off right and left—all of them lined with decrepit two-story frame houses. Grand Avenue was at the top of the hill. The house I wanted, the one that Chard had given as his address, was midway down the block—a two-story frame structure with a dead elm tree in a bed of mulch by the door, like a spade in a freshly turned grave.

I parked the Pinto and walked up to the porch.

There was a lamp on in the front room. I could see it through a seam in the drawn curtains. It was just bright enough to light the mailbox by the door. There was a name tag taped to the box. I glanced at it before I knocked—C. Miller.

A few moments went by and a man I took to be C. Miller answered. He was in his late twenties. Freckled face, red hair, knobby cheeks, with a sparse red mustache and a small tuft of hair growing in the cleft of his chin, like weeds poking through a sidewalk. He was wearing an undershirt and jeans. Through the doorway behind him I could see a chair with a newspaper draped over one of the arms.

"Yes?" the man said. "What is it?"

He had a hole in his mouth where his front two

teeth should have been. It made his voice whistle like
wind in a casement.

"Are you Mr. Miller?"

"Yes, I'm Cass Miller."

"Mr. Miller, I'm looking for Tommy Chard."

The man stepped back, as if I'd insulted him.

"That son-of-a-bitch doesn't live here anymore,"
Miller said bitterly. "He hasn't lived here since spring.
I wish you cops would get that right."

"How do you know I'm a cop?"

The man put his hands on his side and smirked.
"Who else would come around at eight at night looking for Tommy Chard? Everybody knows we aren't
together anymore."

"You're a friend of his?" I asked.

"I used to be, until the bastard robbed me and gave
me this." He pointed to the hole in his teeth. "Once I
filed charges, he ran like a jackrabbit." Miller started to
laugh. "To give the devil his due, Tommy did everything like a jackrabbit."

"You filed charges against him in May?"

"I sure did, sugar. I don't have to stand around and
watch some asshole eat me out of house and home,
spend my money, pawn my goods, and then beat me
up when I tell him to stop. I'm not that far gone yet, I
hope to tell you. I haven't seen him since the day I
called you guys."

"You don't know where he moved to, do you? After
he left here?"

"Try the meat racks. That's all the bastard's good for
anymore. Selling it to the beat freaks down on Plum
and Fourth."

I winced a little, for poor Lessing. "Was Chard into
rough trade?"

"*I* wasn't," Miller said firmly. "But, yeah, Tommy was—professionally speaking. It's how he made pocket money. Every week or two he'd go down to the Ramrod or Fourth and Plum and sell it to some poor john. I knew he was doing it, and I wanted him to stop. But just try and tell Tommy anything. Just try! You end up with a broken nose and a two-thousand-dollar dentist's bill." The man shook his head disgustedly. "I used to pity those freaks sometimes. They just didn't know what they were in for, cruising Tommy T. When that boy was on the rag, he had the devil in him. I'm surprised no one ever got killed."

"Somebody did," I said.

The man paled. "Who are we talking about here?" he said nervously.

"Ira Lessing."

"The Covington councilman?"

I nodded.

Miller put a hand to his mouth and pinched his lower lip until it turned a bloodless white. "You're telling me Tommy had something to do with that?"

"It's possible."

"I thought Terry Carnova had confessed to the murder."

"There's some evidence that Tommy was with Carnova on the night of the killing. They were close friends, weren't they?"

"They knew each other."

The man was choosing his words more carefully now—now that he knew the stakes.

"Did Chard ever mention Lessing to you?"

He shook his head, no. "He didn't tell me about his johns. I never liked to hear that sort of trash, and he knew it. That was for his other friends. His gutter friends."

"Like Carnova?" ·

Miller nodded grudgingly. "Yes."

"Has anyone else ever mentioned Lessing to you?"

"Honey," the man said with a long-suffering look, "there isn't a man or boy who doesn't get mentioned by someone, sometime. We're just like everybody else, we like to claim them as our own."

"What did you hear about Lessing?"

"I never heard he was a beat freak," Miller said, "if that's what you mean. Someone told me he saw Lessing with Terry Carnova once. Of course that was after Terry got arrested for his murder."

"Who said that?"

"Someone at the Underground. I don't remember who."

"Could I find Tommy at the Underground?"

The man shrugged. "He might be there. Or at the Ramrod. Or out on the streets. I really don't know." He sighed. "Tommy was never one to stay put for very long."

"Thanks," I said. "You've been a help."

"To who?" Miller said as he closed the door.

19

. . . .

It was almost nine when I got back downtown. I parked the car in a garage on Fifth and walked over to Fourth—to the Underground nightclub. It didn't look like much on the outside—just a tinted-glass door in a brick wall with a lighted sign above it. As I stood there a young blond kid came out of the shadows on Plum Street. He was about seventeen, wearing a T-shirt and jeans. He gave me a long look, then drifted back into the shadows around the corner.

If it had been a woman hooker, I wouldn't have thought twice about it. But this was a boy, selling himself openly on a downtown street corner—the same corner that Tom Chard worked. They gotta live, too, Harry, I told myself. But that didn't make it any more palatable. I stared at the door to the club, and caught a glimpse of myself reflected in the tinted-glass—a big, sandy-haired man with a pained look on his face.

"Fuck it," I said out loud, and went into the club.

At first glance the Underground looked a lot like any other downtown night spot, except that the only women there were with each other. The room was dominated by an elevated polished-wood dance floor with black, leather-trimmed booths snaking around it and a long parquet bar off to the right. Neon sculptures decorated the black flock walls; a mirrored ball lit by lasers flashed overhead.

The dance floor was crowded with men gyrating to

loud rock 'n' roll. A few of them were dressed like homosexual clichés, in leather vests and leather pants, with motorcycle-chain belts and Harley caps. But there was a lot more Ralph Lauren strutting its stuff than Sonny Barger. A lot of Brooks Brothers too. In fact, the dance floor looked like an undulating menswear department.

Since all the booths were filled with happy couples hooting at the dancers and snapping their fingers to the blare of the music, I moseyed over to the bar. The bartender, a thirtyish guy with a pleasant apple-cheeked face, was filling two pitchers of beer from a tap. He grinned at me as I walked up.

"First time at the Underground?" he said over the roar, as if he'd pegged me for a nellie just coming out of the closet.

Some guys are like that. They're not happy unless you come down with it too. But then it was his turf, and I guess he was entitled to his aspersions.

I said, "Yep, it's my first time."

The bartender smiled at what he assumed were my virgin's nerves. "We're not going to bite you, buddy. The management doesn't allow it."

"Well, that's just swell."

The pitchers started to overflow, and the bartender whisked them away from the spouts, nudging the taps shut with his shoulder. "Let me drop these off, and I'll get back to you."

He walked down to the far end of the bar, balancing the two beer pitchers in his outstretched arms like a man carrying hot rivets in a spoon.

I stood there wishing there was an easy way to find out what I wanted to know. I had to be careful about what I wished for because the guy beside me started brushing against my shoulder like a cat looking to get petted. Once could have been an accident. The second time I wheeled around and pushed him away.

"Back off," I snapped.

He was a little guy in a tailored suit. Tortoise-shell glasses. Crew-cut. A branch manager, maybe.

"Sorry," he said, blanching, and moved up the bar.

"For a fella 'looking for someone,' you've got a funny way of showing it."

I turned back to the bar.

The apple-cheeked bartender was standing there again, grinning his knowing grin.

I'd had it with the smirk. I leaned across the bar and crooked a finger at him. He dipped toward me like a debutante. Up close his breath smelled like Certs and bottled beer.

"I didn't come here to make new friends."

"Well, what exactly did you come here for, butch?"

"I told you I'm looking for somebody."

"Does this lucky devil have a name?"

"Tom Chard. Tommy T. to his pals."

The smile on the bartender's face went round and round, like a spinning bow tie. When it came to a stop, it had turned into a frown. "Are you Vice?"

He was the second guy in a row who had thought "cop" as soon as he heard Chard's name. "Why? Is Tommy T. that bad a boy?"

He didn't answer me.

"I'm not a cop," I said. "A friend of mine knew Chard, and I want to talk to him."

"Then why don't you ask your friend where he is?"

"My friend is dead."

The bartender straightened up, backing away a step and holding his hands out in front of him, palms up, as if he were bringing the conversation to a halt. "Can't help you there, buddy."

"My friend's name was Ira Lessing." I spoke loudly enough so that the people along the bar could hear me.

The bartender folded his arms at his chest and stared at me blankly. If he recognized Ira's name, it didn't show in his eyes. No one else spoke up, either.

"I told you—I can't help you. Now, are you gonna order something or what?"

"Draft beer," I said.

He drew a glass of beer from the tap and smacked it down in front of me. The knowing smile had disappeared and with it the condescending chumminess in his voice. "Find some other house to haunt. Okay? The rest of us are trying to have a good time."

He threw a bar towel over his shoulder and swaggered off.

Even though the room was noisy, a definite silence settled over my spot at the bar. I sighted an empty table and took myself and the glass of beer over to it.

I'd been sitting there a few minutes, watching the beer go flat and trying to brace myself for a trip to the Ramrod, when a guy in a wheelchair rolled up to the table. He was wearing a pea-green fatigue jacket with an Airborne emblem on the right sleeve. Without the braces on his legs he would have been a dead ringer for David Bowie, right down to the funny off-color teeth and the nasty lesbian good looks. He seemed angry, but then being a homosexual vet in a wheelchair would have ruined my day too.

"I heard you at the bar," he said truculently.

I gave him an amused look. "Did somebody appoint you spokesman?"

"Don't get smart, Ethel," he said, pointing a bony finger at me.

"The name's Harry."

"Mine's Vin," he said, wheeling a little closer to the table. "Not that it means a shit."

"What can I do for you, Vin?"

He eyed my glass of beer. "You were looking for conversation, and I could use a drink."

I started to laugh. I guess I hadn't figured on deadbeats cadging freebies in a queer bar. For some reason it made the place seem more human.

"What's so fucking funny?" Vin said in his angry voice.

"Nothing." I swallowed the last of my laughter and pushed the beer glass over to him. "It's been sitting there awhile, but if you want it, take it."

He picked up the glass and drank the beer down in one slug.

"Thanks," he said, just as truculently as he'd said everything else. He dropped the glass back on the table.

I pointed at the emblem on his coat sleeve. "You were Airborne?"

He nodded. "I ain't proud of it. I got caught in the draft and couldn't get 4-effed. Imagine that?"

"Why do you wear the jacket, then?"

Vin shrugged. "I just don't want to look like everyone else in this shithole." He gazed around the room and curled his lip. "Bunch of yuppie faggots."

"If you don't like the company, why come here?"

" 'Cause I'm a faggot too," he said, turning back to me. "If they didn't have so many goddamn stairs to get down, I'd cruise the Ramrod. It's a helluva lot more fun over there."

"How's that?"

"It's more real, that's all. None of this genteel shit."

Vin gave me a knowing look that was a long way
from the bartender's chummy smirk. I didn't know
what to make of it until he told me.

"If you're into rough trade, that's the place to be."

"What makes you think I'm into rough trade?"

"You were asking about Tommy T., weren't you?"
he said cagily.

"You know him?"

The guy balked. "I could use another drink."

I took a twenty out of my wallet and laid it on the
tabletop. "Buy yourself a couple."

"Don't mind if I do." He slapped at the table like a
snake striking at the glass of its cage. The twenty-dollar bill disappeared in his palm.

"Sure I know Tommy," Vin said, pocketing the
money. "I use him myself once in a while."

He smiled as unattractively as I've ever seen a man
smile.

"Where could I find him?" I asked.

"Like I said, Ramrod's your best bet. This place . . .
it's good for a laugh once in a while. But it's just a Girl
Scout troop. Everybody playing patty-cake and showing off their fucking new clothes. Ramrod's a hustler's
bar. That's where you get your hot action. And
Tommy T. . . . well, he's as hot as they get. At least
around this town."

"You wouldn't happen to know a guy named Coates,
would you?"

"That fat pig." He threw his hand at me disgustedly.
"Yeah, I know him."

"I heard he and Tommy were pretty tight."

"Tommy just uses the pig's pad, that's all." Vin

straightened up in the wheelchair. "The T's got better taste than Lester Coates."

"You know where Coates lives? In case I can't find Tommy at the Ramrod?"

"Deco Apartments. Number 425. But don't touch nothing. The stink stays on your hands all day."

I stared at him for a moment—at his nasty lesbian face. "You didn't know Ira Lessing, did you?"

He thought about it for a second. "I seen the name in the papers. The guy that got offed by Terry Carnova, right? The guy you mentioned at the bar."

I nodded. "You ever see him in here with Tommy?"

He shook his head. "Never saw the guy, period. But that don't mean he didn't cruise the bars. Knowing Tommy, he'd more likely be over at the Rod, anyway. That's probably where he picked up Terry, too, the poor fucker."

"Terry was into S and M?"

"Not really. He didn't have the right temperament for the job. Tommy T., he's a cold-blooded cat. Ice cold. But Terry . . . he ain't decided what he is. Hell, I saw him the night your pal got hacked, running around here acting all pissy and tough."

"On the night of the Fourth?"

"About seven o'clock. Shooting his mouth off how it was going to be a big night for him 'cause it was his big-deal birthday. Bragging on how he was going to make a monumental score."

"What kind of score?"

"T's and B's. Christ, he was already loaded. You could see it in his eyes. When everybody got tired of hearing his mouth he went on over to the Rod. Least that's where he said he was going. That's the last time I saw him, till I spotted his picture in the papers.

Guess he scored all right. That friend of yours, Lessing, just picked the wrong boy on the wrong night."

On that note I pushed away from the table.

"Going over to the Ramrod, huh?" Vin said with a touch of disappointment, as if he'd seen the evening developing in a different way.

I nodded.

"It figures. All the good ones go to the Rod." He started to wheel himself away, then turned back to me. "Talk to the bartender—Raymond. Tell him the kind of action you're looking for and tell him Vinnie sent you. You'll be all right."

It's hard to believe, but I actually said, "Thanks."

20

. . . .

The Ramrod was located in the basement of the Lincoln Hotel, three blocks northeast of the Underground. You had to go down a flight of steps off Walnut to get to it—which is what Vinnie had complained about. The walls were stucco instead of flock; the leather trim on the furnishings was red instead of black. Outside of that the setup was identical: elevated dance floor, laser lights, booths, and a mahogany bar. The difference was in the clientele, but it took me awhile to see it.

The clothes were the same—lots of expensive suits and ties, lots of silk shirts and tight pants. The table talk was just as loud, the dancing just as frenetic. But as I sat at the bar, waiting for the bartender to work his way up to me, it dawned on me that, for the most part, there were really only two kinds of people at the Ramrod—middle-aged men and boys in their late teens or early twenties. The boys stood side by side at the bar or strutted together on the dance floor; the men sat at the booths and ogled them. It was exactly like a strip joint—a meat rack, with the boys playing the parts of the B-girls.

Some of the kids were weight-lifter types, steroid freaks with doughboy faces and upper arms that looked like bagged grapefruit. Some of them were thin and nervous, with wiry frames and the mean eyes of speed freaks. A few of them looked all-American as hell, as if they'd just stepped off Wheaties boxes. They all dressed alike, in muscle shirts and sprayed-on pants. They all moved alike, self-consciously, deliberately, as if each one knew he was being watched.

The older men were just as self-conscious—and just as much of a piece. Their suits were tailored, their hair tinted and razor-cut. They wore gold rings, watches, jewelry—anything to make them seem prosperous. They'd affected the look of successful executives, even though half of them probably managed at drive-in restaurants, or kept the books tidy at Blue Cross, or cooked up soap at United American. But no amount of money or flash could disguise the fact that they were buyers in a sellers' market. Their appetites showed through the table talk, the jewelry, the tailored clothes. It gave their eyes the desperate, driven look of obsession.

For all I knew I was staring at a roomful of Ira Lessings. A roomful of Terry Carnovas and Tommy T.'s. The thought was unsettling enough to make me turn back to the bar.

The bartender was standing there waiting for me to order. From the frown on his face, he'd been standing there for a while. There was nothing affable or chummy about this one. In fact, he looked like a piano player in a whorehouse. Thin, flat face. Bee-stung lips. Frog eyes. Pencil mustache. Greasy black hair combed straight back, as if he'd just slid out from under a Chevy. He was probably no more than forty, but he was definitely on his third or fourth lifetime.

"Can I get you?" he said in a weary voice.

"Scotch, straight up."

He poured the drink and set it down on the bar in front of me. I gave him a five.

"Are you Raymond?" I asked.

"I'm Raymond," he said, as if, in Vinnie's words, it didn't mean a shit.

"A guy named Vinnie told me to talk to you."

He still didn't look interested. "Yeah?"

"I'm looking for someone. Tommy T. Vinnie said you'd know where I could find him."

"Tommy hasn't been around all night."

I got another twenty out of my wallet and laid it on the bar.

Raymond smiled dully. "I ain't Tommy."

"I just want a few answers."

He smoothed the twenty out with his right hand, like he was ironing a shirt. "You could try across the street, at the Deco. Sometimes Tommy crashes with a cat who lives there, name of Les Coates."

"I heard that." I studied his face for a second. He still hadn't picked up the twenty. "You ever see him in here with a man named Lessing?"

Raymond laughed—a little blip of a laugh, like a scratch on a record. "You're a reporter, aren't you?"

"Sort of. How'd you know?"

"You're either a reporter or a cop, and I already talked to the cops. Besides, it's been ten years since anyone around here give me a twenty-dollar tip."

"Did you see Tommy T. in here on the night of the Fourth of July?" I asked.

"Saw him and Terry both. Right over there." He pointed to the dance floor. "They left about ten-thirty. One after the other, maybe five minutes apart."

"Was this guy Coates with them?"

Raymond shook his head. "Nope. He wasn't here."

"Did Tommy say where he was going?"

"Nope."

"Did either of them come back in—later on?"

He shook his head again. "That's the last I saw of them that night."

"How about Lessing? You still haven't told me if you saw him here."

"I'm still thinking about it," the bartender said.

"What's to think about? Either you saw him here or you didn't."

"That's big news, huh? If I saw him?"

"It's news."

Raymond put his forefinger on the twenty and began to swivel it around on the polished wood bar. "You know what I don't like about you reporters? You feed on pain."

I laughed out loud. "What do you call this?" I pointed to the hustlers lining the bar.

Raymond looked up at me, still swiveling the bill. "That's not the kind of pain I'm talking about. Besides, we ain't all Tommy T."

He looked back down at the twenty. "Say a guy is basically decent. Good citizen, good provider. Churchgoer, all that. Only he has a kink, a bend. Maybe his old man give him the habit—caught him jerking off and kicked the shit out of him. Tied him down in bed and waited for him to get a hard-on, then scalded him with hot water every night for a year. It happens. Whatever the story, the guy's got a bend that don't straighten out. For the rest of his life it don't straighten out. He goes to shrinks, to whores, to bars. He gets married, has kids. He tries hard as he can to be like everybody else. But he can't be, 'cause of that kink. One night he just can't pretend it ain't there anymore. So he goes out and finds somebody like Tommy T. And maybe that scares him straight for a while. Maybe it don't. Maybe he picks the wrong dude and gets iced."

He pushed the twenty away from him and it fluttered off the bar to the floor. "And that's when somebody like you comes along with a twenty-dollar bill."

Raymond walked down the bar.

"That's it?" I called to him.

"That's it," he said over his shoulder.

It was fully dark when I left the Ramrod. I could have stayed awhile longer, looking for somebody like Vinnie—some barfly desperate for a drink. But I didn't have the stomach for it. I wanted out—back in the real world. Even at that I felt like I was coming out of a porno theater, as if the color on the street was too lurid, the light too intense, the third dimension one dimension too many. Everything looked fat and ripe and repulsive. I knew it was because of the way things had gone with Raymond—because of the way the night had gone up until then, and the way it was bound to go thereafter.

There was no question in my mind that Raymond had seen Ira Lessing in the Ramrod bar. Whether the story he'd told me was something he'd heard about Ira —or just a composite of the lives of other pathetically damaged men—I didn't know. But I felt as if I'd learned a part of Lessing's history in outline, and it depressed me. Even though I'd half expected it, it depressed me. It was something I didn't want to hear.

I stared across the street at the Deco apartment house—a six-story brownstone wedged between a two-story storefront and a ten-story office building. I'd passed the damn thing a thousand times before. It was one of the few downtown residential apartments that predated urban renewal. But at that moment my curiosity was at low ebb.

Instead of immediately tackling Lester Coates, I ducked into a coffee shop at the corner of Seventh and drank ice tea at the counter, in the bright light of ordinary commerce, amid the soothing banalities of a short-order restaurant full of short-tempered waitresses and sweaty natives. When I felt reasonably normal, I went back out onto Walnut, crossed over to the other side of the street, and walked the half block up to the Deco.

21

· · · · · · · · · · · · · · · · · · · ·

The Deco had a buzzer system outside the lobby door
—something I hadn't counted on. That meant I needed
to give Coates a reason to let me in, and the best one I
could think of, on the spur of the moment, was to tell
him I was a cop. I still carried a special deputy's badge
from my days on the D.A.'s staff. If Coates didn't examine it too closely, it might work. And if it didn't
. . . well, I'd be inside by then.

I pressed the button for 425 and a man with an ef-
feminate voice asked, "Who is it?"

I said, "Police, Mr. Coates. We need to ask you a few
more questions about the Carnova case."

"Is this really necessary?" the man said irritably.

"Afraid so."

He pressed the buzzer, opening the main door.

I went in. The place had the look of a dead-end hotel
—grungy green-and-black tile, peeling plaster walls,
bare fluorescent lights overhead. A blue neon sign for
the elevator sputtered at the far end of a hall. I walked
down to it, past the scarred metal doors to the ground-
floor apartments. Someone had put a pottery planter
shaped like a toad on the hall radiator. There were no
plants inside, just cigarette butts and a few condom
wrappers sprouting in the dirt.

Like everything else in the Deco, the elevator looked
grim. It was one of those rickety, self-serve jobs with
graffiti-covered walls and an empty frame where the

safety permit was supposed to be. I got in and pressed four.

While the elevator struggled up to Coates's floor, I read the graffiti. Tommy T's name was etched in one of the walls with the words "The Boss" printed underneath it. Terry Carnova was there, too, inside a heart with Kitty Guinn.

The elevator lurched to a stop on the fourth floor, and I stepped out into a dim hallway with three metal doors opening off it. Apartment 425 was the door farthest from the elevator—the rooms looking out on Walnut at the front of the building. A very fat, very bald man of about forty, wearing a plaid bathrobe, argyle socks, and brown wing-tip shoes, was standing in the open doorway staring at me. He couldn't have been more than five-ten, but his sheer bulk made him look enormous.

"Are you the policeman?" he called out in his squeaky voice.

"Yep."

I took the deputy's badge out of my pocket and walked down to him.

Up close I could see that he wasn't really bald—he'd shaved his head. In fact he seemed to have shaved all his facial hair—eyebrows, eyelashes, beard. It made his fat face look as if it wasn't quite finished, not yet fully human. The tiny blue eyes buried beneath his brow glittered faintly in the hall light.

Through the open door behind him I could see a living room. The furniture—a baize couch and two armchairs—had been beaten to death by the man's bulk. The smell of the room was awful—a greasy odor, mixed with something staler than rotting food.

"You're Lester Coates?"

"Yes. For chrissake, what is it?"

"My name is Stoner." I showed him the badge and he bit his lip. His lips were thick, pink, and sculpted-looking, like soap flowers. "I'm going to have to ask you a few questions."

I edged past him into the living room.

"Questions?" Coates said, scampering up behind me. He must have had taps on the wing tips because his shoes clicked noisily on the linoleum floor. "I've already answered your questions. Why must I do it again? Your Lieutenant Finch seemed content with what I told him several weeks ago."

He'd probably been ecstatic, I said to myself. The last thing Art wanted to do was stumble across another suspect.

I turned around, and Coates hopped away with a pained look, as if I'd stepped on his toe. "We've got some new information we need to check with you."

"About what?"

"About Carnova and a friend of his, Thomas Chard."

"Tommy?" Coates said. "Tommy had nothing to do with it. I've already told you people that. He spent the night with me."

"That's the problem," I said, pretending confusion. "You say he was here all night. But we've got witnesses who'll swear he was with Carnova."

"What witnesses?"

I ignored the question. "We have reliable information that Chard was in the Ramrod up until ten-thirty on the night of the Fourth."

"That's right. And then he came over here."

I shook my head. "He was spotted later that night driving Ira Lessing's BMW—he and Carnova and an-

other boy. All three of them were seen entering your
apartment house early Monday morning. Our witness
says that both Chard and Carnova had bloodstains on
their clothing."

Coates's face reddened. "That's a mistake. Whoever
told you that must be mistaken."

I shrugged noncommittally. "I guess we've got a
problem, then. Maybe you'd better get dressed, Mr.
Coates."

"Dressed?" he said, taking a step back.

"We'll go down to the Justice Center and try to clear
this thing up."

The man pursed his florid lips, as if he didn't like the
taste of that at all. "I'm not going anywhere with you.
This whole thing is ridiculous."

I gave Coates a tough look. "Get your clothes on and
let's go."

"I'm not leaving here!" the man said, stamping his
feet like a hysterical child. His taps rang on the tile.
"You have no right to detain me."

"If you withhold evidence in a murder case, you're
an accessory to murder, Mr. Coates. That gives me a
right."

"Accessory," he said, staring at me, horrified.

"You could be opening yourself to a lot of charges.
Concealing evidence. Conspiracy. Obstruction of justice. Aiding and abetting. Perjury. Homicide."

Coates flinched a little each time I ticked off a
charge. When I finished, he dropped his head to his
chest.

"Enough," he said in a strangled voice.

Head bent, he walked over to the couch and dropped
heavily onto the cushions. He put his hands on his

knees and sat there for a second, staring dully at the far
wall of his horrible room.

"I can't go to jail," he said, as if that was the one
thing that had become clear to him. "I'd die in jail."

I didn't say anything.

The man cleared his throat and looked up at me miserably. "If I talk to you, I won't go to jail?"

"Not if you tell the truth."

"The truth?" Coates echoed, as if the word was new
to him. "All right. I'll tell the truth."

I took a notebook and a pencil out of my coat.

Coates cleared his throat again and made a show out
of straightening the hem of his robe above his fat white
knees. "I . . . I didn't really spend the whole night
with Tommy. I was confused before. Shocked by the
murder. And then Lieutenant Finch was only interested in Terry."

"I understand," I said.

"Tommy and I are very close, you know," Coates
said with a pathetic smile.

"When *did* Tommy come to your apartment?"

"Around one A.M., I think. It may have been later
than that."

"Who was with him?"

"Terry Carnova and another boy, Terry's cousin. I
don't know the other boy's name. They were all rather
high. And Terry seemed very nervous."

"Did they make any reference to Ira Lessing?"

Coates shook his head decisively. "No. I'd never
heard of Lessing before he was murdered. And neither
of them mentioned him that night. Tommy said they'd
been in a fight with some blacks on Ninth Street.
That's why their clothes were . . . soiled. I offered
him a change of clothes—I keep a few of his items in

the bedroom. While he was changing, Terry and his cousin left."

"Chard stayed that night?"

Coates nodded.

"What did you do with his bloody clothes?"

Coates put a hand to his brow, shading his eyes from mine. "I washed them out for him, as well as I could. But the stains on the shirt were quite heavy."

"You don't still have these items of clothing, do you?"

Coates didn't say anything for a moment. He just sat there with his hand to his brow.

"Mr. Coates?"

"Tommy took the pants. The shirt . . . he burned the shirt in the incinerator." He sighed so heavily that his whole body shook beneath the robe.

I had the feeling that it was Coates who had burned the shirt, but there was no way to prove it.

"That clothing was evidence in a murder, Mr. Coates. You may have opened yourself to a very serious charge."

The man dropped his hand and looked up at me with a desperate plea in his eyes. "But all I did was help a friend!"

"You aided and abetted a felon. You concealed evidence."

"No!" he said, his voice rising hysterically. "You don't understand. It was false evidence. False! And Tommy is no felon. He didn't do it. Terry did."

"Were you there?"

"Of course not," he said, looking appalled.

"Then how do you know what happened on the night of the Fourth?"

"Because Tommy told me he didn't do it," he said with conviction.

I gave him a hard look. "What did he tell you?"

"I . . ."

"You can do it here. Or you can do it downtown."

Coates ducked his head tragically.

"He told me Lessing was a friend of Terry's," he said in a defeated voice. "Lessing had picked Terry up in front of the Ramrod that Sunday night. About an hour later Tommy saw Terry driving the BMW on Fourth Street, flagged him down, and got in. Lessing wasn't in the car anymore, but there was blood everywhere. That's how Tommy's clothes got stained. He asked Terry what had happened. And Terry said that he'd killed the man and left his body by the river. Terry was too keyed up to drive, so Tommy took the wheel. They picked up Terry's cousin and came over here. After Terry left, Tommy found the car keys in the living room. He didn't want to leave the car in front of my apartment—it would have incriminated him. So he drove it to the Union Terminal lot early Monday morning and abandoned it there."

The man wiped the sweat from his eyes. "I believe him," he whispered. "That's why I lied."

I didn't know what to believe. It was exactly the opposite of what Kitty Guinn had said and exactly what you'd have expected Chard to say in his own defense. The only thing that seemed clear to me at that moment was that it wouldn't have taken much to set either boy off.

"We'll still want to talk to Chard, Mr. Coates."

"Of course," he said. "Of course you do."

"And we're going to need your testimony regarding the shirt."

Coates cringed. "But I care for Tommy."

"Enough to go to jail for him?"

Coates didn't answer. He didn't have to.

I got up from the couch and walked over to the door. "You think about it, Mr. Coates."

I could have gone back to the Ramrod—or staked out the Deco on the off chance that Chard would show up. But I'd had enough of Tommy T.'s world for one night. I went home—to the apartment on Ohio—downed a couple of scotches, lay down on the living room couch with an ice pack on my head, and tried not to think about the Lessing case.

But I couldn't relax. It was partly the feel of the apartment, still new to me, still too much like rented rooms. The exposed brick walls, the beamed ceiling, the bay window winking in the headlights of the traffic on Ohio. There was no place for my eyes to rest, nothing familiar, nothing with a history to it. My mind kept drifting back to Lessing and those two feral boys.

Who was to say who'd actually done the killing? Carnova or Chard? For all I knew O'Brien was right and Lessing had arranged it himself. Perhaps Ira had become addicted to the ugly, ambivalent thrill, like Raymond the bartender had speculated. Perhaps he himself had pushed one of those two lethal punks to the limit on that hot July night.

I didn't know. I wasn't sure I ever would. But I could no longer kid myself that Ira Lessing had been a straight arrow, victimized purely by chance. He'd picked one or both of those kids up. I'd have been willing to bet that he'd done the same thing many times before—driven by whatever fire was raging inside his own mind and body, by the fire raging inside those two feral boys. And that night he'd been unlucky. That night he'd been consumed.

22

. . . .

The late summer heat woke me early the next morning. I hadn't slept well anyway, wondering what to do about Chard. I thought about going to Finch. But without a piece of solid evidence to back my story, I knew that Art would let the thing slide, just as he had months before when O'Brien had first approached him with Kitty Guinn's story. Without proof my suspicions were nothing more than hearsay speculation, and no D.A. in his right mind would jeopardize an iron-clad case to follow up on something like that.

On the other hand, Jack O'Brien would be more than happy to use my information, whether I had proof or not. In fact, with a few subpoenas and a little luck, he might be able to parlay it into a scandal. All he needed to do was establish a reasonable doubt that Carnova had done the killing. If a jury could be made to believe that there might have been a second suspect whom the cops hadn't bothered to pick up, Carnova's doctored confession would be worthless and Carnova himself might walk. I didn't want to see that happen any more than I wanted to see Chard go scot-free—not until I knew what really took place on that July night.

That left the Lessing family. I was sure they'd be eager to see justice done to Ira's killer. The trouble was that Chard was a homosexual sadist, specializing in beat freaks, and I was just as sure that the Lessings would be far from eager to hear that.

From talking to O'Brien and DeVries, I already

knew how hard I an and the family had worked to
keep the homosexual gossip out of the spotlight. In
fact, up until the night before, I'd conspired at the
same thing. If Chard was indicted, all that work would
go down the drain. Lessing's homosexuality would become the pivotal point of the case, and the Lessings
would once again be caught up in personal and public
nightmares.

Any way I looked at it, someone was going to suffer
because of what I'd come across the night before. Like
Naomi Trimble, I'd faced the truth and asked the hard
questions. No one had said I'd like the answers. And I
didn't.

It was too early in the morning to try to pick up
Chard's trail again, even if I'd had a taste for it, which
I didn't. Instead I decided to try to drum up a little
support from a neutral corner—someone who cared
enough about Lessing to want to find the truth and
who was close enough to the family to argue the case
against Chard for me, if I could make the case stick.
There was only one person I could think of who fit
that bill, Commissioner Don Geneva, the Lessing family spokesman. After breakfast I drove over to Kentucky to see him.

It was just a little past ten when I parked in front of
the battlements of the Covington Court House. I
snaked my way through the crowd of lawyers and liti-
gants in the lobby, past the tubby, sullen security
guard, up to the second floor. There was a black
wreath on the door to Ira Lessing's office. I'd never
been inside that office. And that was something else
Geneva could help me with.

I found the sleek-looking Mr. Geneva two doors up,

talking earnestly to an attractive blond woman who was sitting on a corner of his desk. They both stared at me when I tapped on the doorjamb.

"Can't talk to you right now, fella," Geneva said brusquely. "If you need to see me, make an appointment with the secretary down the hall."

"I can't wait for an appointment," I said. "It's about Ira Lessing."

The woman looked mildly shocked, as if I'd used a rude word. But Geneva sat back slowly in his chair.

"You're the detective, aren't you? Stoner?"

"I'm surprised you remember the name."

Geneva smiled a slick smile. "It's a trick you learn as a politician. Mnemonic devices. You got a hard-looking face—a little knicked up. So I think of stone."

He glanced at the blond woman, who was taking a second, more appreciative look at my stonelike face.

"Gloria, you think we could postpone this for a while?" he said to her.

She glanced back at him and nodded. After collecting some papers from the desk, the woman walked out of the room. She smiled openly at me as she went by, shutting the door behind her.

"I think she likes you," Geneva said with a grin.

"I'm flattered."

"You should be. Gloria's considered a major catch around these parts." He gestured to the chair across the desk from him and I sat down. "Now what about Ira?"

"I need your help."

"Doing what?"

"Finding his killer."

Geneva looked as shocked as I'd wanted him to be.

"They arrested his killer months ago. That little creep Carnova."

"A second kid may have been involved. A boy named Tommy Chard."

"I haven't read anything about a second suspect in the papers or heard anything about it from Meg or Len."

"That's because I haven't told the papers or the Lessings yet. I'm telling you."

"I don't understand. What do you have to do with it?"

"It's a long story."

He leaned back in the chair and locked his hands behind his neck. "Let's hear it."

I went through the whole thing for him: Jack O'Brien, Kitty Guinn, Naomi Trimble, Kent Holliday, Vinnie, Raymond the bartender, and Lester Coates. The only thing I held back was the fact that I'd witnessed Carnova's first confession, the one with the homosexual accusations in it. He was a lawyer, so he grasped some of the problems without having to be told. What he didn't understand was why I hadn't gone directly to the family.

"I'm sure they'd like to know there's another suspect. Jesus, the last thing they'd want is to let Ira's killer go free."

"You understand that Chard is an ugly character—a homosexual prostitute specializing in masochists."

"Carnova was hardly an angel."

"This is different. This is something the family and the D.A. won't be able to sidestep."

For the second time since I'd met him I watched Don Geneva's jaw slowly drop as he came to grips with what I was saying. Momentarily, he was at a loss for words. "You believe it, then," he finally said in a shocked voice. "You believe the Carnova kid's accusations?"

"I don't know if Lessing was a beat freak. But, yes, I think he was homosexual."

Geneva shook his head. "You're wrong. I knew Ira well, and he was as straight as they come."

"Look, Geneva, *you* don't have to believe Lessing was gay to help me. But if I don't get your cooperation, I'm going to have to pursue this in some other way that may end up hurting the family or jeopardizing the case against Carnova."

"You could just let it go," he said with a lawyerlike edge in his voice. "You could do that."

"Yeah. But then Chard walks and Carnova fries for something he might not have done."

"Let me make a few calls," Geneva said. "Talk it over with Meg and Len. Personally, I will never believe that Ira Lessing was anything other than a decent, respectable, and very straight man. But if this pervert hijacked him and murdered him for his money, I think they'll want him punished, even if the publicity stinks."

"Fine," I said.

"I'll call you later today, and we'll see what can be done."

"One more favor?"

He nodded.

"Can you get me into Lessing's office here at the Court House? I'd like to see if he left anything behind that might connect to this. It would help a lot if I could come up with some physical evidence linking Lessing to Chard."

Geneva fished a key chain from his pocket and tossed it across the desk to me. "The big silver one opens every door on this floor."

"Thanks," I said, pocketing the keys.

23

. . . .

I went back up the hall to Lessing's office and slipped
the silver key into the lock. The door opened and a
wave of heat came flooding out, like the very breath of
that murderous summer. I walked over to the far wall,
cracked a window, and let the room air out for a second. Then I flipped on an overhead light and went in,
closing the door behind me.

It was identical to Geneva's office. Oblong, lined
with bookshelves on the two long walls, and tall fan
windows opposite the door. A desk stood in the center
of the room, as tidily arranged as the desk in Lessing's
business office. I sat down behind it and stared at a
picture of Janey sitting on one corner. There was a
picture of his mother on the opposite corner. Meg Lessing looked as stern as Janey looked careless, like the
two poles of the man's life.

I opened the top drawer of the desk and went
through it. I could tell from the way the items were
neatly arrayed that nobody had searched the desk before. But that didn't surprise me. Once Finch and the
D.A. had settled on Carnova as the murderer, every
other possibility had been left unexplored. Hell, I'd
confirmed that the night before, in Coates's grim little
apartment.

I found some pens and pencils in the top drawer, a
squared-up ream of stationery with Lessing's name
embossed on it, an address book. Nothing important. I
opened the side drawer and found another squared-up

ream of stationery and a shiny leather Dopp Kit with shaving gear and a manicure set inside—all as neat as a pin. At the bottom of the drawer I found a wooden presentation box with the name Thomas Lessing engraved on a bronze placard. Inside the box, nestled in plush velvet, was a chrome-plated .38-caliber revolver —a presentation piece that had obviously never been used, perhaps never touched. It was the only memento of his father that Lessing had kept in either office—a chrome-plated pistol.

There were a couple of neatly stacked piles of papers on the desk pad. I thumbed through them listlessly. Reports to a committee. Queries about various items. A note from Geneva.

Idly, I reached across the desk and pulled the flip calendar over to me. It was still opened to July 4, like a clock that had stopped at Lessing's death. And right there, on the part of the page ruled for the evening hours, was written in tiny, perfectly formed letters: "Birthday/C."

I stared at the damn thing for so long I lost track of the time. Then I began to go back through the calendar, page by page. There were countless daily appointments with men and woman whose names I didn't know. Appointments and meetings so carefully documented that he'd often broken the hours down into five- and ten-minute segments. When I got to June 15, I found another "C" notation in the 11:00 A.M. slot: "Car Tune-Up/C." I had a feeling that was the day that O'Brien had said the service manager at Riverside BMW had seen Carnova in Lessing's car. I flipped back to June 3, the date of the check I'd discovered in Lessing's other office, and found a missing page. It had been torn off the calendar, omitted from the record as if the day hadn't happened in his life.

I went back farther, but couldn't find any more "C's." Just page after page of minutely detailed appointments. Every hour of every day accounted for. Every obligation, right down to Carnova's birthday. Everything but that one day in his life—June 3.

Lessing's obsession with putting it all down, with keeping it neat, had told me more about his secret life than he'd wanted known. But the very ferocity with which each day was mapped out said something else— something that could only be read in the light of what had happened. This was a man trying desperately, through the most minute arrangements of his time, through the piling on of obligation and appointment, to keep each hour of each day under strictest control.

The missing day, the third of June, was the puzzler. I'd found other notations stretching through August, into that hot, cruel month when he was already dead and his homosexuality was being exposed in the press. Only the third of June didn't exist for him.

I'd never followed up the chance meeting with Kingston at the cemetery. Never bothered to find out who had brought in the Lighthouse checks Lessing had pinned to his other calendar—the checks dated the third of June. I'd thought Finch would handle it. Now it seemed worth looking into on my own.

I relocked the office door, dropped the keys off with Geneva, and walked down to the car. It took me ten minutes to drive uptown to the clinic, past the bars that had so upset Ira Lessing—the bars with the teenage prostitutes.

It must have been a special day at the Lighthouse

because a number of kids were lined up on the sidewalk outside the door. I parked the Pinto and made my way through the crowd. A couple of strung-out teenagers gave me nasty looks, as if I were breaking line at a theater.

Inside, the nurse stationed at the reception desk was taking down names and directing kids through the swinging doors to the infirmary. It took me a few minutes to catch her eye.

"Yes?" she said, looking harried. She was the same girl I'd met on my first trip to the clinic—the one who'd been upset by the screaming kid.

"My name's Stoner," I said to her. "You might remember me. I worked for the Lessing family."

She nodded. "Yes, I remember you."

"You think I could talk to Dr. Kingston?"

"We're pretty busy."

"It's important," I said.

"All right, I'll see."

She got up from the desk and went into the clinic. The boy at the head of the line—a tall, skinny teenager with the heavily lined, haunted-looking face of a middle-aged drunk—shifted his feet and stared angrily at me, as if I was keeping him from his fix. A moment later the nurse reappeared.

"Go on back," she said to me.

I went through the doors into the infirmary. Kingston was waiting just inside. Behind him, on the far side of the room, another group of kids were lined up in front of the window of a dispensary, where an attendant was handing them paper cups.

Kingston saw me looking at them.

"Methadone," he explained in his husky, wised-up voice. "All those people who want to legalize drugs

ought to pay a visit to this place around eleven in the
morning." He looked down at the floor. "I haven't seen
you since the funeral, Stoner."

"A lot's happened since then."

"Yes," he said somberly. "I've read about some of it.
I suppose everyone in town has." He started to say
something else—about the allegations, I thought—but
held off.

"What can I do for you?" he said instead.

"You remember those checks I gave you?"

He nodded. "The ones I handed over to the cop back
in July."

"Do you think I could talk to your bookkeeper about
them?"

"Don't see why not, although your cop friend already has the story."

"Finch came back?"

"Right after the funeral. He spent an hour with
Marty."

"I'd still like to talk to her."

"Right this way."

He led me across the room, past the line of junkies to
a door marked "Staff Only." There was an office inside, with a barred window looking out on a sunlit
alley behind the clinic. A small, dark-haired woman
with half-frame tortoise-shell glasses on a nervous,
owl-like face was sitting at a desk totaling figures on an
adding machine. She peered at us menacingly over the
half-frames as we came in.

"I'm pretty busy, Sam," she said.

"This is Harry Stoner, Marty," Kingston said, as if
she had said nothing more than a polite hello. "He
needs to ask you a few questions about those checks we
gave to the cops. The ones from Ira Lessing."

The woman tapped her forefinger on the desktop. "I've been through that with the police."

"Would you mind doing it again?" I said with a smile. "It could be important."

She took off her glasses and tossed them on her desk. "Fine," she said disgustedly. "I'm made out of free time."

I sat down across the desk from her, and Kingston ducked out the door.

"Look, I've got a lot of things to do so let's make this quick," the woman said, putting a hand to her brow and massaging her forehead. "Ever since Ira Lessing died I've been up to my ears in work."

"Why is that?"

She dropped her hand and stared at me incredulously, as if she couldn't believe my gall in asking the question. "We've had to scramble for contributions if you really need to know. And I'm the one who does most of the scrambling."

"Lessing was a great supporter of the clinic, wasn't he?"

She nodded. "He had a thing for disadvantaged kids. Judging from the papers, he had a thing for kids, period."

"You believe the gossip?" I said, surprised that she'd admit it.

"I always felt there was something odd about him," she said matter-of-factly. "Sam couldn't afford to see beyond the charity. Well, maybe that's not fair—he genuinely liked Lessing."

"You didn't?"

"I liked him fine," she said. "I'm just a little suspicious of human goodness. I can believe it about dogs and cats. But human beings . . . Five years at a drug rehabilitation clinic does that to you."

It hadn't done that to Kingston, but then he was clearly a different sort of character than Ms. Levine.

"About the checks?" I said.

"Not much of a story, really. A young guy brought them in on the morning of June 4. I happened to be working the reception desk that day, otherwise it might've gone unnoticed."

"What might have gone unnoticed?"

"The signature on the checks wasn't right. I mean, it wasn't Lessing's. We've had kids try to pass bad paper on us before, so I called Lessing at the Court House. At first he was confused, but when I told him the name of the kid with the checks, he said to go ahead and accept them. We did, and the kid entered the program. At least he signed up and got a week's worth of free methadone. As far as I know we never saw him again after that."

"And what was the kid's name?"

"Well, he wasn't really a kid. I'd say he was twenty, twenty-one. And his name . . ." She opened a cardboard file box on her desk and flipped through the cards. "His name was Chard. Thomas Chard."

I stared at her for a long moment. "You told the police that?"

"Months ago."

"Did you ever figure out who'd endorsed the checks?"

"Lessing called back about a half an hour after I'd called him and said that his wife had endorsed the checks for him the day before—he'd simply forgotten about it."

"So Janey Lessing gave Chard the checks?"

"I guess so," Marty Levine said. "You'd have to ask her to be sure."

That was what I intended to do.

24

. . . .

I stopped in Kingston's office carrel before leaving—to
see if he could tell me anything more about Chard.

"I don't really remember him that well," he said.
"He only came in once."

"Was he alone when he came in?"

"As far as I remember he was. Why the interest?"

I didn't want to go through it with him—not until I
had proof. So I said, "I'm just tying up some loose
strings."

I could tell from the look on his face that he didn't
believe me. But he must have been used to being lied to
because all he said was, "Glad we could help."

"Do you remember what Chard's problem was?"

"T's and B's, I think. He didn't really want to kick
the habit. He just wanted access to free medication—
like a lot of them do. We gave him a physical, blood
tests, the whole nine yards. He never came back for the
results."

"T's and B's. That's what that kid was high on the
day I first came here."

"They're a poor man's version of base. Talwin and
blues—Pyribenzamine. The one's a painkiller, the other's antihistamine. Mixed together they're dynamite.
Kids combine the capsules one to three, one to four.
Sometimes they break the caps, cook the stuff up, and
shoot it." He stared through the glass of his cubicle at
the raggedy line of strung-out teenagers standing in

front of the dispensary. "That bastard Carnova. He shot the stuff regularly."

"I take it T's and B's can have a violent effect."

Kingston nodded. "Very violent, like angel dust. Sometimes kids will attack their friends, sometimes they mutilate themselves."

"Carnova was high on T's and B's the night of the murder."

Kingston got a pained look on his face. "That would explain the brutality of the crime. If he was high enough, he probably didn't even know what he was doing."

"I think he knew what he was doing," I said to the doctor.

"Yeah, I've read those stories too. And we've been hearing the same crap from some of the kids on the street."

"You don't believe them?"

Kingston leaned back in his chair and stared at the clutter of papers on his desk. "Ira Lessing was a good man. I'll never think any less of him than that. But where is it written that a man's goodness isn't just as complicated as every other part of his life? Who can look into anyone's heart and find . . . perfection? Who could say that about himself?"

"No one."

"Damn right," Sam Kingston said.

It was almost noon when I pulled up on Riverside Drive beneath the pretty French Quarter house on the hill. I got out into the sun and walked up the flight of steps to the terrace. There was a water glass half full of whiskey sitting on the tile by one of the cane chairs. It should have told me something about the mood inside.

Instead, it made me thirsty. I wasn't looking forward to what I had to do.

I knocked, and a few moments later Janey Lessing answered. Her pretty little-girl's face looked chalky and careworn, aged as if by illness. She stared at me for a moment without reacting, as if I wasn't really there. I thought perhaps she'd forgotten my name, but when she held that dead-eyed stare awhile longer, I realized she was drugged or drunk. When I stepped closer to her I could smell the liquor on her breath.

I said, "Do you remember me, Mrs. Lessing?"

"You're the detective." Her voice was flat and weary —not at all like the anxious, pouty-little-girl voice I remembered.

"You think we could talk?"

"Why not?" Janey said. "I still talk, when someone will listen."

She waved me through the front door.

I followed her down the hall with the Impressionist prints to the too-white living room with its red Rothko blazing above the fireplace. Janey went directly to the liquor cart and poured herself a drink. A glass of booze was already sitting on the coffee table in front of the couch, but the girl didn't notice it, like a person lighting a second cigarette when the first is still burning.

"You want a drink?" she said to me.

I shook my head, and she laughed sarcastically. "Too early in the day?"

She came around the side of the couch and sat down across from me.

"I drink a lot now," she said in that flattened-out, emotionless voice. "It's the only thing Len and I share anymore, except for a morbid interest in my mental health. Which, as everyone will tell you, isn't very good. I'm not . . . what is it Meg says? I'm not making the adjustment." She drained half of her drink and let her head loll heavily against the cushions. "What do you want, Mr. Stoner?"

"I need to talk to you about a boy named Tommy Chard."

"I don't think I know anyone named Chard."

"You gave two checks to him about four months ago."

"Chard?" she repeated curiously. "What were the checks for?"

"They were made out to the Lighthouse Drug Rehabilitation Clinic."

She took another sip of the drink. "It couldn't have been very important because I don't remember it."

She certainly didn't sound as if she was lying, but then she'd had a lot to drink and the past few months had clearly taken their toll. "Maybe if you think back to that day—June 3?"

The girl smiled gruesomely. "I don't much like thinking back. It's getting harder and harder to remember what I did an hour ago. These damn pills I take . . . they're supposed to cheer me up, but what they really do is make me forget. You know, the weirdest thing is that I don't dream anymore. Why is that? I can't seem to remember my dreams."

"About the third," I said, trying to get her back on track, even though it looked hopeless. "Your husband didn't have any appointments that day. Is it possible that he was out of town?"

"We were here in June," she said matter-of-factly. "There was nothing special. What day did you ask about?"

"The third."

"I can't remember anything."

She took another sip of whiskey and stared at me blearily. "Aren't you enjoying our talk, Mr. Stoner? Most people get that look on their face after two or three minutes with me. You've lasted . . ."

She turned her wrist to look at her watch and spilled the drink she was holding into her lap. Her face flushed with embarrassment.

"Oh, Janey's made a mess," she said with a wretched laugh. "Maybe I've had enough." She swiped viciously at the ice cubes, knocking them on the floor. "Maybe Janey shouldn't drink—that's what Meg and Ira say." She flushed again. "Did I say Ira?"

I looked away, at the floor.

"Isn't that the oddest thing? But there's a point to it. There's a point to little slips, they tell me. I guess what I was really saying was that I feel guilty."

"For what?" I said, looking up at her red, ravaged face.

"For what happened to Ira," she said. "They all blame me, anyway."

"They?"

"Meg and her crew. They blame me. I mean they don't say it, but they do. Isn't that why you're here—to blame me?"

She was a little right. She was also a little crazy and quite drunk now—so drunk she had trouble sitting up.

"I'm here to find out what happened to Ira."

"What happened to him?" she said with a single laugh that racked her like a sob. "Anyone can tell you what happened to him. He's dead. He was here and now he's gone. It's what happened in between that we don't talk about. We do drop hints, though, from time to time. Mostly we act as if there was something Janey should have done. *What should Janey have done?* Like an assignment in school."

She struggled to keep her eyes focused on me. "You know, it's probably a defect in my personality—lack of initiative. I didn't dare ask questions when I lived at home with my father. And when I met Ira, well, I was so grateful to be taken away that anything he did was all right with me. Even when I knew he wasn't happy —and he wasn't, despite what Meg says—I didn't ask him why. I didn't think I was supposed to. Can you blame someone for that?"

"No one blames you," I said.

She gave me a disgusted look. "Now you sound like Len." Janey picked up the other glass of whiskey from the coffee table and drank it down. When she started talking again her concentration failed. "I shouldn't have let him leave—that night. I knew . . . I knew something would happen."

"Why?" I said. "Why did you think that?"

Her eyelids fluttered, as if she was going to pass out. "Because he told me something was going to happen," she whispered.

The second glass fell from her hand onto the rug. This time she didn't notice. Curling up on the couch, she closed her eyes.

A moment later she was passed out.

25

. . . .

I checked the girl's pulse after she passed out. Her heartbeat was strong, but I wasn't sure what other drugs she might have taken along with the booze. To be on the safe side, I phoned Trumaine at the plastics shop.

"Jesus," he said with alarm. "She knows she shouldn't drink while she's taking those damn pills."

"What pills?"

"Elavil. It's an antidepressant."

"Maybe we better call a doctor."

Trumaine hedged. "I'll come over. Give me ten minutes."

While I was waiting for Len to arrive I got an Indian blanket from one of the upstairs bedrooms and covered the girl. She looked a lot less troubled asleep than she had awake. But then she didn't dream when she was asleep.

What she'd told me about herself and Ira had been disjointed, skewed by the pills and the booze. But it was obvious that the guilt she felt over Lessing's death was destroying her. Kitty Guinn had claimed that guilt stemmed from the fact that Janey had known about her husband's homosexuality. But judging from what I'd heard that morning, I wasn't sure Janey had known Ira's secret until after he was dead. It wasn't unusual in a case like this for one spouse not to know, or not to want to know, the other's guilty secret, especially if the spouse was as childlike and devoted as Janey had apparently been.

Obviously the girl had guessed that something was wrong—Lessing himself had told her as much on the night he was murdered. Apparently he had known full well he was headed for disaster, and the girl had understood enough of his mood to react hysterically to his subsequent disappearance. But she hadn't understood the full meaning of it—or if she had, she'd kept it entirely to herself during the long, nerve-racking week after his car was discovered in the Terminal lot. Given her fragility and her devotion to the man, I had trouble seeing her do that, although I supposed it was possible.

I wished I'd had the chance to question her fully about what Lessing had told her on that hot July night. I wished she could have told me something about the third of June—that blank day in Lessing's charted life. But the answers to those questions would obviously have to wait until a time when Janey could face her own life without Elavil and Johnnie Walker Black Label.

Precisely ten minutes after I'd called, Len Trumaine came rushing into the living room with an anxious look on his drooping, moony face. He walked over to the girl and felt her cheek, then gently combed the loose blond hair from her forehead.

"Do you want to call a doctor?" I said.

He shook his head. "It's happened before. She'll be all right. It's the stress—some days it just overwhelms her." Len looked up suddenly, as if talking about stress had made him realize that I shouldn't have been in that room. "What are you doing here, Harry?"

I told him the truth. "I was asking Janey about a kid named Tom Chard."

Trumaine stared at me, slack-jawed. I knew at once that he recognized the name, and from the stricken look in his eyes, I realized that he knew about Chard's reputation too. What I didn't know was where he'd heard it.

His face reddened, almost as if he'd guessed what I was thinking. When he spoke his voice was angry, defensive. "You have no right to mention that bastard to Janey. Christ, you didn't tell her anything about him, did you?"

"No," I said.

"Because that's all we need," he went on, almost hysterically. "I mean she believes everything she reads about Ira or hears on TV, anyway. She absorbs it like a sponge and turns it into guilt. Blaming herself for not knowing. Blaming us for not acting to save him. Blaming the world for not seeing what wasn't even there. If she thought Ira was mixed up with that psychopath, I think she'd go right over the edge."

"Where did *you* hear about him, Len?"

He flushed again. "Finch mentioned him once," he said. "A few weeks ago. Carnova's lawyer had some ugly theory about this Chard and Ira. Finch didn't buy it. I didn't either. Why do you care?"

"Because I think Chard may have been involved in Ira's murder."

"That's ridiculous," he snapped. "Carnova confessed to the killing. He didn't mention any accomplice. And what the hell would Janey have to do with it, anyway?"

"Chard got two checks from Ira early in June.

Money to pay for rehabilitation at the Lighthouse Clinic. Janey apparently endorsed the checks."

"I don't believe it," Trumaine said flatly. "She never endorsed Ira's checks."

"Someone did."

"So what? Maybe Millie did it—she'd sign checks for both of us on occasion. So the kid had a couple of checks. Ira handed out money all the time. He was a charitable man."

I hadn't wanted to get into it with him because I'd known how he'd react. I guess I should also have known that he'd be familiar with Chard. After all, he'd spent almost two months working closely with the police, the D.A., and everyone else associated with the case. Months spent trying to ensure that this very issue —the question of Lessing's homosexuality and the bearing it had had on his murder—wouldn't become the focus of the trial. He was protecting the family. He was protecting his friend. He was trying to keep the girl sane. But looking at the angry embarrassment written on his face, hearing the defensive tone in his voice, knowing that he'd tried to bribe O'Brien into laying off the beat-freak issue, I didn't believe that Len still thought that Ira Lessing was the chance victim of a homicidal teenager.

I didn't say that. It would have made him that much more defensive. Besides, I liked the man too much to call him a liar.

"Len, I'm not trying to hurt you or Janey or the family. But there are reasons, good reasons, to think that Carnova didn't act alone."

"You can prove that?"

"I have some evidence pointing to Chard. None of it conclusive."

"Then for God's sake drop it, Harry. For *her* sake. She can't take more bad news. It'll kill her."

The girl stirred on the couch and Len shuddered nervously. "She's worn out," he said, looking panic-stricken. "Can't you see that for yourself?"

"You don't care, Len, that Chard will walk away?"

"I care about this." His hand hovered above Janey's face. "She's had a horrible life, Harry, except for the past few years with Ira. You don't understand how horrible."

"I'm sure the last two months have been tough."

"That's not what I mean." He took a deep breath, as if he were summoning his strength. "Look, if I tell you something about Janey, will you promise never to repeat it?"

I didn't particularly want to have my sympathies played on. But the man obviously wanted to talk me out of going any further, and I was more than a little curious about the Lessings. So I said, "You have my word."

"Janey's father . . ." Len's face got very red. "He abused her."

"Janey was sexually abused as a child?" I said, feeling sorry that I'd heard it.

He nodded unhappily. "A young child."

"Did Lessing know that?"

"From the start. Almost by instinct. On that very first night I introduced them, he knew. We talked about it later on, when we were driving back to school, and he'd guessed it all."

"Perhaps he'd already had some experience with parental abuse," I said, thinking of what Raymond the bartender had said.

"I've wondered about that myself, seeing what a

heartless bastard his dad was. And over the last few months . . . well, you can't help thinking all sorts of crazy things. But if it *was* true, Ira never told me or anyone else I know. If it was true, he kept it inside of him and concentrated on work and charity and Janey."

"That would have been in character, wouldn't it? Keeping it inside?"

"Jesus, Harry," Len said in an outraged voice. "Do you have to turn it all against him, even his pain? If you could have seen how gentle and kind he was to Janey, how patient and understanding . . . He gave her a sense of identity, without making any demands on her strength. He let her escape her past." His face flushed guiltily and he ducked his head. "I couldn't ever do that."

"Why not, Len?"

He wouldn't look at me. He didn't answer, either, for a long time.

"Because I was part of it," he finally said in a terrible voice. "I knew about Janey's dad and I never told anyone. She didn't want me to. She was afraid, and I . . . I was afraid for her."

"You can't blame yourself for that."

"Oh, can't I?" he said with a horrible laugh. He plucked at his tight-fitting shirt, at the layered flesh underneath it, as if the fat were something he wore in penance for the past. "I will never stop blaming myself for that. I let her down when I was all she had. I'll never do that again. This time I'll fight for her. I swear it."

I stared at him, at the angry, shamefaced schoolboy that had emerged from inside him. "Forget it, Len," I said. "It won't come to that. You have my word."

. . . .

26

I had a much better picture of the Lessings now, wife and husband. I even had a lead to follow—Millie the secretary, who sometimes signed the checks for Mr. L. I hadn't actually shown her the checks the day I took them from Lessing's office; it was possible she'd endorsed them—or knew who had. And Lessing & Trumaine was no more than a few blocks away. But it was just too far to travel to find out the truth about Tommy Chard. At least that was the way I felt at that moment.

I headed back across the river, back to the city. On the way I thought about Trumaine, a fat, unhappy kid who'd grown into a fatter, unhappier man because he'd blown his one chance at love, because, at the age of ten or eleven, he couldn't muster the heart to speak the unspeakable.

And now I wasn't going to speak it either. I knew it as I drove away from Riverside Drive. There had been too much unhappiness visited upon all the actors in the Lessing case, victims and persecutors alike. The extenuating circumstances kept extenuating, further and further back into each one's past, until the lines converged in lonely childhoods where there wasn't any love to be found. That wasn't the kind of damage I could fix or that a court could settle. Chard would get his due, inevitably. But not this day, not this case, not by me.

I parked in the underground garage on Fifth Street and walked back to my office. I knew I was going to have to call O'Brien sooner or later. But before I did that I wanted to pay Naomi Trimble a visit. She'd done a brave thing, a dangerous thing, coming to see me. So had her cousin Kent. I owed her an explanation of why I was backing off.

I found the tag of paper with her address on it in the top drawer of my desk. She lived on State, in the heart of the Appalachian ghetto. It was a short drive, and I had nothing but time on my hands that afternoon.

The house on State was a few doors up from the iron fretwork of the Elberon overpass. I parked on the west side of the street, in the heavy noonday shadow of the viaduct, then walked across to number 310. It was a frame one-story bungalow, sided in shingles, in a block of frame bungalows built on the sloping bias of the street. The shades were drawn in the two front windows of 310 and in the tiny window of the door. I stepped up on the stoop and knocked. No one answered.

Naomi Trimble had said that she worked nights, so I figured she was probably asleep. As I stood there on the stoop a woman in a floral housedress, her red hair wrapped in a scarf, stepped out of the door of 312 and stared at me with naked curiosity. She had a blotchy alcoholic's face, puffed up around the eyes and collapsed at the cheeks where her back teeth had been pulled. She was probably in her mid-thirties, but hard drinking had turned her into an old woman.

"Y'all looking for Naomi?" she said, putting a hand to her brow to shield it from the sun.

"Yes, ma'am."

"You a bill collector?"

"A friend," I said.

The woman smiled a salacious, broken-toothed smile. "A friend, huh? Well, I don't think she'll be seeing no friends this afternoon."

"Why is that?"

"She run on out of here after that guy come to see her 'round nine this morning. They had some words, I can tell you! Heard them shouting from next door."

"What guy is this?"

"Don't know his name. Just a young guy—good-looking but kinda mean. I seen him around the neighborhood a couple times. Used to pal with Terry Carnova and that bunch of no-goods."

It didn't have to be Chard, but it certainly sounded like him. I stared nervously at Naomi's door. "Do you know when she's coming back?"

The woman shook her head. "Way she was worked-up, she may *not* come back."

"Great," I said under my breath. To the woman I said, "Would you tell her Harry Stoner stopped by? Tell her to call me."

"Stoner," she repeated. "I'll do that."

But I had my doubts. In a couple of hours the woman probably wouldn't be able to think about anything except hitting the glass with the bottle.

When she went back in I took a pencil and a piece of paper out of my notebook, wrote down a short message, saying I'd stopped by and would come back later that evening, and left it in the door.

I took Ninth Street back to town, then went south on Vine to the underground garage again. After parking the car I walked down to the Tri-City Building and Jack O'Brien's office.

When I knocked on the door to the suite, O'Brien himself answered.

"Secretary's gone to lunch," he said, looking a little embarrassed at having to act as his own receptionist. "I was grabbing a bite myself, back in the office."

"Have your lunch."

"Fuck it," O'Brien said miserably. "I don't feel like eating."

"What's the trouble, Jack?"

He shook his head. "You don't want to know."

I followed him into the inner office. O'Brien sat down behind his desk and stared at a half-eaten corned-beef sandwich sitting on a paper plate in front of him.

"I love corned beef," he said wistfully.

I smiled. "What the hell ruined your appetite?"

"Terry Carnova called me in for a conference at the Justice Center about an hour ago. I thought it was going to be more of the usual bullshit. You know, the guards aren't treating him right, the other prisoners are giving him a hard time—that sort of thing. Instead, he tells me he wants to plead guilty to all charges. He doesn't want me to put up a defense of any kind. He particularly doesn't want anyone else implicated in the Lessing murder. There wasn't any question who he meant, either. Because when I tried to argue him out of it by telling him that his pal Tommy T. was going to laugh at him when he went to the electric chair, he said that was the way he wanted it. Chard had had nothing to do with the murder; it had been between him and Lessing from the start."

"Isn't that what he's always said?"

"Yes and no. He'd begun to loosen up a little over the last few weeks. To tell me a few things about his relationship with Lessing. You know—to humanize it and himself."

I gave him a grim look. "Just how did he manage to do that?"

"Don't start with me, Stoner," O'Brien said irritably. "That man you're so fond of defending was a fucking weirdo. Maybe he wasn't always that way. Maybe he was a great guy in his off time. But not on summer nights. Not after this spring."

"What happened this spring?"

"Terry said Lessing changed," O'Brien said. "Before the spring he was just a guy looking for somebody to hold hands with—some kid he could play daddy to. Then something must have happened to him, something that really screwed him up, because by June he was a completely different kind of cat—sick, snarly, looking to get hurt. That's what Terry said, anyway." O'Brien stared disgustedly at his corned beef. "I was just winning that kid's confidence. Now . . . it's like day one. All he wants to do is get the thing over with and take his punishment."

"Do you have any idea what changed his mind?"

"The fact that he got a visit from Tom Chard around eleven this morning should tell you something."

"You think Chard threatened him?"

"I think he's been threatening everybody. I tried to talk with Naomi Trimble early this morning, and she wouldn't say a word about Chard or Terry. And I haven't been able to get hold of Kitty Guinn since last night."

"They've always been afraid of Chard, Jack."

"Yeah, but this is different. It's like Chard's suddenly gone on a rampage, like something's set him off." He stared at me curiously. "It doesn't have anything to do with you, does it?"

I'd toured Tommy T.'s world the night before, asking questions, stirring up trouble. If the kid had come back to the Underground or the Ramrod or gone to visit Coates later that night, he would have heard about me wherever he stopped.

I said, "It might."

"Does that mean you're onto something?"

"Nothing solid, Jack."

O'Brien got a belligerent look in his eye, as if he intended to grill me about Chard, then gave it up with a sigh. "Aw hell, what do I care? It was a lousy case anyway. I don't know why I got so worked up about it to begin with. I guess twenty-five years of rewriting wills and probating estates makes you a little trigger-happy when you finally do get something with flesh on it. We'd have been lucky to get Terry off with twenty-to-life."

"So you're going to plead him guilty?"

"What choice do I have?" O'Brien said. "The trial starts next Monday."

27

I brooded about what O'Brien had said on my way uptown to the Riorley. If Carnova had decided on his own to plead guilty, I wouldn't have cared. In fact, given the situation with Len and Janey, I might have been relieved. But the fact that he'd been intimidated into doing it by Chard—and that I was part of the reason—bothered me a lot. It bothered me even more that Chard had apparently threatened Kitty Guinn and Naomi Trimble.

Tommy T. had probably been feeling pretty safe up until the night before, when I'd come barging into his world, asking leading questions. I hadn't really tipped my hand at the two bars, but I had with Coates. I'd frightened the man badly, and I'd made him betray his friend. He might have felt guilty enough afterwards to seek Chard out and tell him that a cop was on his tail. After two and a half months of feeling safe, Tommy T. could well have had a violent reaction to that kind of news.

I told myself that Chard wasn't my business any-more—that I'd made a decision and I'd have to live with it. But the whole thing left a taste that I knew wasn't going to go away for a long time to come.

Around four that afternoon I got a call from Don Geneva.

"Look, Stoner," he said, "I'm afraid I'm not going to

be able to help you with this Tom Chard business after all."

I should have told him that it didn't matter, but I didn't. Instead I asked, "Why?"

"The family doesn't want any more complications. If you had solid evidence, it might be different. But as it stands, they don't want me to get involved."

"They?"

"Meg, actually. I couldn't get hold of Len. She was . . ." He cleared his throat noisily. "She had a very bad reaction to this thing. It surprised me a little."

After what Janey had said it didn't surprise me at all. It was clear that Meg and Len were the powers behind the cover-up, and that, for different reasons, each one was prepared to sacrifice the truth to avoid further scandal.

"That's all right," I told Geneva. "I'll handle it on my own."

"Stoner, I wouldn't if I were you," he said, suddenly sounding very much the lawyer. "You don't have any right to involve yourself in this matter. In fact, your interference could constitute illegal tampering."

"Jesus Christ," I said with a bitter laugh. "Are you threatening me?"

"I'm stating the facts as the family sees them."

"All of this because her kid was gay?"

"Just stay out of it," Geneva said, losing his cool. "You don't have the right to pass judgment on them. Or on him."

He hung up with a bang.

It was just about quitting time when I got the second call. In fact, I'd closed shop fifteen minutes early, gotten the office bottle out of the desk, and begun to drink. I drank to take the bad taste away. But it wouldn't wash out; it kept getting worse.

When the phone rang I was feeling mean enough to say just about anything to anyone. As it turned out I didn't do very much talking.

It was Jack O'Brien. I could tell from the traffic noise in the background that he was calling from an open-air phone booth. And it was clear from his voice that he was upset.

"Stoner, could you come over to . . ." He went off the line for a second, and I heard someone else talking excitedly.

"I'm sorry," he said when he came back on. "The address is 4678 Baltimore. Can you get over here right away?"

"Why?" I said, lifting the glass of booze to my lips.

"It's Kitty Guinn." A truck rumbled past him on the street, and I couldn't hear what he said next.

"Say again?"

"I said she's dead," he shouted over the roar of the truck.

"Dead?" I put the glass down on my desktop.

"So is the other kid."

"What kid?"

"Kent Holliday."

It took me about twenty minutes to make it to Baltimore Avenue in South Fairmount. I didn't have any trouble finding the right address—there was an ambulance in the driveway and patrol cars up and down the block. Guys in work clothes, just home from second shift, their anxious-looking wives, their excited kids, were standing on porches, staring fixedly at the doddering frame two-story with all the cops inside it. I parked three doors up and walked back down to the crime-scene barricade.

This was a working-class neighborhood. Peeling frame houses, fields full of auto parts and flat tires, little squares of yard going bald or to weeds. It was a far cry from Riverside Drive, and the cops at the barricade didn't give much of a damn who came and went as long as they looked semiofficial. I managed to get past them by flashing my ersatz special deputy's badge.

I went up a cracked walkway to the porch and found Jack O'Brien leaning heavily on the railing, head down, tie loosened, shirt unbuttoned at the neck. It was hot in the setting sun that poured over the gray slat veranda, but it wasn't hot enough to make a man look like O'Brien looked. He'd obviously been sick, but then he wasn't used to violence. He was used to probates and wills.

"It's a horrible mess inside," he said, swallowing hard.

I stared at him coldly. "Was it Chard?"

"No one knows. They're questioning Kent's aunt, Naomi Trimble, right now."

"She's inside?"

"The cops picked her up after I phoned Station X."

"You found the bodies?"

He nodded grimly. "After I talked to you I had an attack of conscience and drove over here looking for Kitty. I thought maybe she could talk Terry out of pleading guilty." He stared ominously at the door, lit up by the sunset. "I don't know how I'm going to break the news to him."

I stared at the door too. It opened on a narrow, unfurnished hall.

"You going in?" O'Brien said.

"I think I better."

I stepped through the door into the hallway. There was a stairway to the left and a living room to the right. The living room was where the trouble had been. It was where the cops were now—a half dozen of them sifting through the broken furniture and the blood.

I didn't go into the room itself. I could see all I wanted to see from where I was standing.

The two bodies were still lying where they'd fallen. The girl was collapsed on a threadbare floral-print couch, head thrown back, her red hair streaming down over the cushions. She'd been shot in the mouth. The concussion had broken her front teeth and burned her tongue almost black. There was a great deal of dark clotted blood in her hair, on her lips, and down her pale neck. She held a rusted Colt .38 in her right hand.

The boy was facedown on the floor, directly across the room from Kitty Guinn. He'd been shot several times in the body. Judging by the bullet holes in a spindle-legged coffee table and the blood smears on the hardwood floor, Kent had tried to hide from the bullets. At the end he'd apparently grabbed a heavy glass ashtray and held it over his head—like a shield. He was still holding it to the crown of his head in death, like a glass coronet. It lent an absurd edge to the frightening carnage inside the room.

I went back out onto the porch, feeling stunned. The kid had been all redneck, so had the girl. Neither one of them had had much use for me—or for each other— but they'd both shown courage and street smarts when it counted. At least they had up until that afternoon.

O'Brien stared at me searchingly. "What do you think? I mean about . . . in there?"

I glanced at the street, squinting into the sun and all those other fixed faces staring back at me. "I don't know, Jack. It looks like a murder-suicide. Of course it could have been made to look that way." I turned to him. "I know she didn't like Naomi or Holliday, but did she hate him enough to kill him?"

O'Brien ducked his head. "Yesterday I told her what you told me," he said in a guilty voice. "About Naomi coming to see you, about a witness who could implicate Chard."

I thought about that for a second. "So let's say Kitty figured my witness was Kent. That's certainly no reason to kill him and then kill herself."

"She's been pretty crazy the last few days, Harry. The phone threats and the pressure of testifying at the trial—they'd unhinged her. I told you that—I told you she was right on the edge. Paranoid as hell and swallowing every drug she could find."

"That was normal, wasn't it? The drugs?"

"What I mean is she was at the end of her rope mentally. I knew it last night when I talked to her—I could hear it in her voice. I guess I shouldn't have told her about Naomi Trimble. I knew the girl didn't like her or Kent. But I was getting near the end of my rope too." He slapped his right hand against the side of his leg. "Christ, I might have caused this thing."

"I can't buy that," I said, maybe because I was feeling guilty too. Because if O'Brien had had a hand in it, so had I.

"I don't know, Harry," Jack said, shaking his head. "If Chard was planning to kill Kitty, why did he go to see Terry this morning? I mean, why did he bother to threaten Terry if he was planning to carry out the threat?"

"Maybe Chard *wasn't* planning to carry out his threat. Maybe something happened to change his mind this afternoon."

"Anything's possible," Jack said without conviction.

It was obvious that he didn't buy my theory. Maybe I didn't buy it, either. But I sure as hell was going to check it out.

28

. . . .

I waited on the porch with O'Brien for the cops to finish with Naomi Trimble. If Kitty had had a murderous grudge against Kent Holliday, the older woman would have known. And I wasn't about to accept the murder-suicide scenario until I'd heard her confirm it. Even then I didn't know if I could buy in. I just had too many other reasons to blame Chard.

The sun set while we waited—one of those spectacular purple and orange parfaits, half the work of Indian summer, half smog alert. As night came on the crowd of onlookers melted away into their homes. Lights popped on in curtained windows; the crickets started up in the surrounding woods. It would have been a typical September evening in South Fairmount if it wasn't for the two bodies lying on the floor inside Kitty Guinn's rented rooms.

The neighbors must have heard what had happened by then because a hush had literally fallen over the street. There were no whoops from kids playing night games, no racket of lawn mowers or chatter of televisions on front stoops. Just the crickets and the cops and the cop radios.

Around nine Naomi Trimble came out the front door. By then we'd heard from one of the investigating officers that the time of death had been set at around 4 P.M. We'd also heard that the police had tentatively decided to treat the case as a murder-suicide.

Naomi had obviously played a part in their decision,

and I wanted to hear what she'd told them. But it was plain from the blasted look on her face that I wasn't going to get the whole story. What became even plainer as we talked was that she was scared almost witless. By the murders, obviously. But also by Chard.

"Can't talk no more," she said when I pulled her aside. "I can't."

"Just a few questions, Naomi."

She put a trembling hand to her cheek and stared at me with something like horror. She was no longer the same woman who'd come to my office—the heart had gone out of her. "Shouldn't have never come to talk to you, Mr. Stoner," she said. "Shouldn't have never done it."

"Did Chard do this?" I asked.

"I ain't talking about him," she said in a fierce whisper, as if she didn't want the cops to overhear. "This all come down 'cause I talked too much, trying to save that no-good son-of-a-bitch Terry. Now Kent is dead." A sob racked her, but she choked it down immediately, swallowing it like medicine.

"Why is Kent dead?" I said to her.

" 'Cause you shot your mouth off about him and me to that bitch Kitty," she whispered bitterly. "That crazy bitch. I warned Kent last night to steer clear of her. He had damn good reason to steer clear of her."

"What reason?" O'Brien said.

"Didn't she threaten to kill me yesterday?" the woman said, outraged. "And Kent, too, if he didn't go down to the courtroom and testify. She knew damn well we couldn't do that. She was just as scared as we were of testifying."

"Because of Chard?"

"It don't matter because of what. Kent's dead and I

did it to him." She backed away, shuddering up and down and tossing her hands at us as if we'd been holding her back physically. "I'm getting out of here. I gotta go."

She walked quickly off the porch and down to the street. I watched her get in a beat-up Plymouth Sebring and drive off.

I had the sure feeling that Naomi Trimble was running from Chard as well as from the burden of Kent's death. She was terrified by what she'd seen in that living room and by what she thought might be in store for her. I felt partly responsible for that—I felt responsible for Chard.

She hadn't even mentioned him to the cops. Which, in itself, was telling. She'd kept Tommy T. out of it, according to a young detective named Forrest, whom I spoke to after Naomi left. O'Brien and I spent the better part of an hour trying to talk him into picking Chard up. But Forrest was a rookie who wasn't prepared to make a decision on his own—not without evidence, which neither of us could supply.

By half-past ten Forrest had gone, too, leaving O'Brien and me alone on that dark, depressing street.

"What the hell are we going to do?" Jack said as we walked to our cars.

"*You're* going to call Art Finch."

"Hell, he's part of that damn Lessing mob. He won't do anything—certainly not for me."

"Call him anyway. These murders don't jeopardize his case against Carnova. He might play ball."

O'Brien thought about it for a second, then nodded.

"All right, I'll call him. What about you? What are you going to do?"

"I think it's time I met Tommy T."

It was almost midnight when I dropped back into the Ramrod bar, down the single flight of steps off Walnut Street, through the padded leather door into that noisy, flashing, desperate bit of hell. If Raymond the bartender recognized me, he didn't show it. I ordered a double scotch, straight up. He poured it from a flute-nosed bottle and smacked it down on a paper coaster.

"Two bucks," he said in his world-weary voice.

I gave him a five. "Seen Tommy T. in here tonight?"

"Not yet," Raymond said as he strolled away.

I took the drink to an empty table in a dark corner of the room, away from the dance floor and the laser lights. A few of the well-dressed older men gave me vaguely sinister looks, as if they thought I might be competition. A couple of the younger ones sauntered past, strutting their stuff. Whatever they read on my face, nobody sat down. And after a while nobody came near.

I sat there for almost two hours, drinking scotch and waiting. I thought about crossing the street to the Deco and leaning on Coates again. And then, around two, just as Raymond made the last call, Tommy Chard came through the door.

It was something to see—how they made way for him. The old guys and the young ones too. As if he were some kind of demonic royalty. The prince of this darkness. He made a triumphant progress down the bar, getting openly stared at, occasionally talked to, never touched. He stopped in the center and raised two fingers to Raymond, who poured him a double vodka. He tossed it down like tap water and turned to face the room, parking his elbows on the bar.

If he had a guilty conscience over the two dead kids on Baltimore Avenue, it certainly didn't show in his face or his manner. And I knew that he wasn't worried about being picked up by the cops or he wouldn't have come to the bar. Either he hadn't heard about the deaths or he hadn't been directly involved. Or he just didn't care—any more than he'd cared about Lessing's murder.

I studied Tommy T. for a few minutes. He didn't look any different than he had in the mug shot I'd seen —a tall, muscular, menacing kid with a dirty angel's face, like something mean and vain and pretty stamped on a bronze coin. He couldn't see me from where he was standing. But then he wasn't looking around. He knew where his audience was—the ranks of frail, frightened, preening men in the leather booths, the shoe clerks and the bank managers. The Ira Lessings.

The pickings must have been lean at that hour of the night because the kid looked away, almost disgustedly. He had a thin, ivory knife scar on his right cheek—an old wound that hadn't shown up in the mug shot. He ran a finger down it twice, tracing it as if it were something he wanted to remember, to remind himself of, to remind the room of. He dug a wad of money out of the back of his jeans and peeled off a ten.

He had quite a lot of money, and he flashed it openly, as if it, too, was something he wanted the world to see. Raymond made change for him, and the kid stuck it in his pocket.

Pushing away from the bar, he gave the older men one long, haughty look, then started back up the bar

for the door. After a moment I got to my feet and
followed him out.

He was half a block south on Walnut when I reached
the street. I gave him another few seconds before I
started after him. He went straight down Walnut, in
and out of the glare of the arc lights and the neon of
storefronts, disappearing into the thick shadow of a
tall office building arcade, then reappearing in the
spotlight of an all-night garage. He walked deliberately, at a leisurely pace, without looking left or right,
as if he knew exactly where he was headed.

At Fourth Street he turned east. The sidewalk was
darker there, canopied by storefront arcades and the
board-and-pipe tunnels of fresh construction work.
The city was building a new tower on the block—a
naked concrete-and-steel superstructure, strung on the
unfinished floors with bulbs and plank fencing. They
were hard at work at that hour—the riveters—high
above Fourth. Their din hit the street like a bag full of
chains—a jangling, metallic crash, like the end of the
world.

Chard kept going, through the roar, still heading
east. The noise from the construction work faded away
as we got to Broadway. It was a part of town that
would never be torn down for reconstruction—the
part with the men's clubs and the old-money apartment houses with Greek Revival facades. Chard had no
business in that neighborhood, but by then I knew he
wasn't there to stay. In fact, I thought I knew exactly
where he was heading.

And sure enough, he turned south past the Univer-
sity Club into Lytle Park.

It wasn't really a park at all. Just a posh gaslit lawn,
with a statue of Lincoln at the west end and the Taft

Museum at the east. In the daytime it was a pictur-
esque spot, surrounded by those genteel apartments
and fancy clubs. Late at night the bums came up from
the riverfront to sleep on the benches. And the hustlers came out to be cruised.

It wasn't Chard's territory—Fourth and Plum was.
But maybe he'd gotten tired of the downtown trade.
Maybe he was looking to move up in his world.

Chard walked over to a bench beneath a gas lamp
and sat down. I hung back in the shadow of an apartment house and watched him. He might have killed
two kids that afternoon. He had probably killed Lessing two months before—or watched his pal Terry do
it. And now he was waiting for someone else to hurt.

It didn't do anymore to tell myself that pain was
Tommy T.'s business—that Lessing had wanted, perhaps invited, what he'd gotten. It didn't do to tell myself that I had no solid proof—with Kent and Kitty
dead, no proof at all. Trumaine, poor Janey Lessing,
they didn't enter into it, either. This was between me
and that kid.

I stepped out of the shadows and started across the
street. I'd just entered the west end of the park when a
car came up Fourth and stopped in front of the boy on
the bench. The kid stood up, walked over to the driver's door, opened it, and got in.

The car idled for a moment, in a cloud of exhaust,
then began to move west. I ducked behind the statue
just as it passed.

I couldn't get a good view of the man who was sit-
ting in the passenger seat. But it was sure as hell a red
Volvo with Kentucky plates—the same car that Len
Trumaine drove.

29

If I'd had a car of my own, I would have followed them.

But I didn't have a car, so all I could do was stand there in the shadow of the statue, in the feeble moonlight, and feel the dread start in the pit of my stomach. There was no doubt that what I had witnessed had either been a casual pickup or a prearranged rendezvous. I knew Len Trumaine well enough to rule out a pickup. So if it *had* been his red Volvo, that meant Len had deliberately sought Tom Chard out. Worse, it meant he'd known where and how to find the kid. I didn't want to think about what that might imply—not until I was sure it was Len in that car, not until I'd confronted him with what I'd seen. But if it was Trumaine hunkered down in the front seat, then something was very wrong with the Lessing case—something had likely been wrong for a long time.

I tried to swallow the feeling of dread as I walked back uptown. But it stayed with me, deep in my gut—a feeling that it was out of control, that it had been out of control from the start, that I'd been playing in the dark all along.

It took me about fifteen minutes to get back to Walnut Street and the Deco apartment house. I couldn't think of anyplace else to go—anyplace else where I'd have half a chance of finding Chard before the night was out. The Ramrod was closed at that hour of the morning, so were all the other bars, gay and straight.

But a light was on in Coates's fourth-floor-front window. I could see it plainly from the street. Either Lester was already entertaining or he was expecting company—and that gave me some hope.

I settled in the shadow of the doorway of a jewelry store, catercorner to the Deco, and waited.

An hour passed, very slowly. I stamped my feet to ward off fatigue. I chain-smoked until I'd made a tepee of butts between my feet. I read the prices off the items in the jewelry-store window. I read a brochure on term life insurance I'd found lying on the pavement. I studied the Deco itself until I knew every line of its facade, from the crenels on its rooftop to the fire escape zigzagging down its south wall.

But by four-thirty I was beginning to run out of patience—and steam. After what I'd seen in Lytle Park, I knew I was going to have a long day ahead of me, and I wasn't going to be good for anything unless I got a few hours rest. I was thinking about going back to the Riorley and catching some sleep on the office couch when I got lucky.

Walnut was dark on the east side except around the Deco's front entrance, where the pavement was lighted. So I didn't spot him until he was almost at the door. But as soon as he stepped into the light, I could see that the man walking down the sidewalk was Chard. He was still grinning that vain, pretty, malevolent grin. There was no sign of the red Volvo.

I glanced at my watch, which was showing four forty-five, then back at the door. There was no sense in making a run at him. He'd be in the lobby before I got across the street—or halfway down the block. And I was in no shape to catch a twenty-year-old kid on foot.

No, it was better if he went in and up to Coates's apartment. I stood a good chance of cornering him there if I could take him by surprise.

As I was thinking it out Chard pressed the buzzer, and a few moments later Coates let him in. I gave him a few more seconds to clear the lobby, then stepped out into the streetlight, crossed Walnut, and walked down half a block to the small dark alley running between the Deco and the office building to its south.

I had to jump a couple of times before I caught the ladder to the Deco fire escape. It swung down with a rusty creak that echoed up and down the alleyway. I stepped onto the first rung and started climbing.

The thing was rickety and it was dark between the buildings. Twice I stepped in planters that tenants had placed on landings outside their windows. By the time I got to the fourth floor my eyes had adjusted to the scarce moonlight and the first dim light of dawn.

The fourth-floor landing ran virtually the length of the building, from the bedroom window of Coates's apartment to the living-room window of the apartment in the rear. From where I was standing Coates's window was about ten feet away.

Very carefully I walked the short distance to the bedroom window. Crouching down, I peered around the brick wall into the bedroom. A light was on on a bureau across from a walnut bed and bedstead. There was a desk to the right, with a fan buzzing on it, and a door opposite the window, probably leading to a bathroom. To the left was the door leading to the living room. It was closed.

Coates had left the window open a crack—wide enough for me to get a grip on it and slowly push it up. I hoped that the buzz of the desk fan would cover whatever noise I made, but the window opened easily. A moment later I was standing beside the bedstead.

Like the living room, the place smelled of rotted food and unwashed flesh. Here and there Coates had hung photographs on the wall—of him in a mortar board and graduation gown; of a fat, smiling older woman with a sad look in her hooded eyes; of a young Lester Coates dressed in a business suit, eighty pounds lighter and ages younger than he was now. Over the bedboard, high on the wall, a twisting, tormented Jesus was daily dying for poor Lester's sins.

I went over to the living-room door and put an ear to one of the panels. I could just barely hear conversation over the buzz of the fan on the desktop. Nobody was shouting. Nobody was upset. And that was good.

I took the Gold Cup out of my shoulder holster, cocked it, unlocked it, and stepped back. With the pistol in my right hand, I gripped the doorknob with my left, turned it, and pulled the door open.

They were sitting right across from me, on the beaten couch—Coates nearest to the bedroom door, Chard on the other end of the couch next to a floor lamp. I stepped into the room, pulling the door shut behind me.

Chard leapt to his feet. He would have bolted for the door if I hadn't been holding the gun on him.

Coates stared at the kid with astonishment.

"What?" he said in confusion. Then he looked over his shoulder at where Chard was looking. When he spotted me he clapped a hand to his fat, repulsive mouth and whimpered out loud.

The kid's angel's face turned into a mask of rage. The transformation couldn't have been more startling or complete if he'd actually sprouted horns from the

knobs above his eyebrows. He bared his teeth like a
cornered animal and growled at Coates:

"You've done this to me, you fucker! You set me up!"
His voice had a feral edge to it—a sharp, unappeasable
ferocity, like the snapping of teeth.

Coates started sputtering. "Tommy, I didn't. I swear
on all the saints I didn't!"

The fat man hopped to his feet with that astonishing
agility that some fat men seem to have. He turned to
me and raised his arms, as if in prayer.

"Please, tell him," he said, coming at me with a desperate look on his face. "Tell him I didn't do it!"

"Stand away!" I shouted at the fat man.

But he kept coming.

I stepped to the right, out of Coates's path. But the
kid was on the move too. As I struggled with Coates,
Chard came up behind him and whipped his right arm
at the back of Coates's bald head. I saw the glint of
metal, and then the fat man's heavy-lidded eyes literally popped open. Coates clapped both hands on the
back of his head and shrieked—his face melting with
terror and pain. He took one of his hands away from
his head and stared at it in horror. The palm was covered with blood. His eyelids fluttered and his flesh
turned white.

"Oh sweet Jesus!" he cried, and collapsed against me
with a groan.

"Get off me, you fat son-of-a-bitch!" I shouted, trying to push him back.

Before I could free my arms Chard whipped his left
hand into the floor lamp, knocking it over. The bulb
went out with a blue flash, leaving the room in darkness. I heard the kid scramble across the tile. A second
later the front door flew open, and an ingot of hall

light fell onto the floor like a dead weight. Chard was through the doorway immediately and down the hall.

I managed to push Coates off me. As he slumped to the floor I ran across the room into the hall. But by then Tommy T. was down the staircase, on his way to the street. I stood in that peeling hallway, listening to his footsteps in the stairwell, and cursed at the top of my voice:

"Goddamn! Son-of-a-bitch!"

Nobody on the floor even opened a door. Not for me or for Lester, who was still groaning in the living room.

I locked the automatic, holstered it, and walked back into the dark living room. I could just make out Lester's bulk on the left side of the room. I could smell urine, where Lester had wet himself. He was groaning steadily. I stepped over him and opened the bedroom door.

I glanced at the tormented Jesus above the bedstead, then went over to the desk, picked up a phone, and called an ambulance.

30

. . . .

I managed to find a light bulb in the bathroom closet and a towel to stanch Coates's head wound. By the time the life squad arrived Lester was sitting up on the living-room couch—the bloody towel pressed to the back of his head, his bathrobe reeking of piss. He'd recovered enough of his composure by then to think ahead, and the one thing foremost in his mind was Tommy T.

"I've got to get out of here," he said with dismal lucidity as one of the paramedics put a compress bandage on the back of his head. "I've got to leave town."

"You gotta go to the hospital first," the paramedic said grimly. "That's a razor cut, and it's deep."

Coates laughed feebly. "He carries a straight razor in his pocket."

"Who does that?" the other paramedic said.

Coates didn't answer him. Instead, he looked directly at me. There was blood smeared on his cheeks and down his robe and neck. "He knows about you."

"You told him?"

Coates nodded. "Something else. He's going to leave. I don't know why, but he said he was going to leave soon. He's getting money. I don't know from where, but he's getting a lot of money, and he's going to leave."

"You still think he didn't have anything to do with Lessing's murder?"

"What difference does it make what I think?" Coates

said with a bitter laugh. "I wouldn't live long enough to say what I think. He thinks I've betrayed him and he'll kill me." His mouth began to tremble. "I've got to get out."

"Just calm down, mister," one of the paramedics said.

"Two kids were killed this afternoon on the west side," I said to Coates. "Kent Holliday and Kitty Guinn."

Coates looked shocked. "I know them."

"Chard made threats against both of them."

"It wasn't Tommy," Coates said defensively. "He was with me this afternoon."

"I've heard that before, Coates."

"Christ, why would I lie about it now! I was with him."

I stared at the man—at his blood-smeared, exhausted, hopeless-looking face—and knew that he wasn't lying, not this time. I also knew that it didn't make a difference. Chard might not have done the actual killing, but he'd driven the girl to it. And I'd let it happen.

I caught a few hours sleep on the office couch, enough to keep the staggers away. Around eight I got up and drank half a pot of coffee. It was too early to call O'Brien—to see if he'd gotten anywhere with Finch. But it wasn't too early to stake out the plastics shop. I grabbed my sport coat from the rack by the desk and started out the door.

It was another misty morning, sticky and hot, with the promise of fiercer heat later in the day. I'd already broken into a sweat by the time I pulled up to the door of Lessing & Trumaine. I got out of the Pinto and walked over to the fenced lot. Trumaine's red Volvo was parked in the back, in the stall with his name on it.

I went around to the front of the building and into the anteroom. Bronze-haired, chatty Millie was sitting at her desk, typing on her word processor. She looked up at me and smiled.

"Long time no see," she said in her jangly voice.

"Long time," I said. "Is Len in?"

"Nope. He came and went."

"His car's outside."

"Mrs. L. picked him up about ten minutes ago. Mr. T. said they had to go on over to the lawyers' to settle up some of Mr. L.'s estate." Her face fell when she mentioned Lessing. "I still get sad every time I think about it."

"Did Len say when he'd be back?"

"Around noon, I think."

I sat down on the chair across from her desk. "I guess I'll have to catch him after lunch."

"Well, don't expect him to be real friendly," Millie said acidly. "He was in here before I was this morning, looking like he slept in his clothes and acting mean and nasty. He stayed that way till he left."

There was a chance that he *had* slept in his clothes, just as I had. And spending part of the night with Chard would have ruined anyone's mood. "Did he say why he was upset?"

"You think he'd ever tell *me* the whole of it?" she said scoffingly, as if Len were her own unruly child. "He'll just fume and bark at every little thing till he works it out of his system. Like this morning he was all p.o.'d 'cause I don't have the accounts caught up from last week, when he knows darn well I've been busy with the inventory. Then, to top it off, he starts asking me fool questions about some checks I signed from four months ago." Millie literally threw up her hands in disgust. "Now how the heck am I supposed to get the accounts caught up if I gotta take time out to go over the books from four months ago?"

I didn't know if the Lighthouse checks had led to the meeting with Chard, but I'd mentioned them the day before—and Len had claimed that Millie had signed them, rather than Janey.

I said to the girl, "I might have put that check idea in Len's mind. Remember those checks I took from Mr. Lessing's desk, the ones made out to the Lighthouse?"

"It wasn't *those*," Millie said flatly. "I didn't have nothing to do with those."

"You didn't sign those checks?" I said with surprise.

"Heck no."

"Then which checks was Len talking about?"

Some of the high jinks went out of Millie's face. "Mr. Stoner, I don't know if I should talk about it," she said, sounding secretarial.

I tried smiling at her. "It'll stay between us."

"I don't know," she said again.

"Look, Millie," I said, putting a bit of urgency in my voice, "Len may be in a bind. I'd like to help him out. But I need your cooperation."

She ducked her head. "I signed some checks for Mr. L., back in May."

"When in May?"

"Starting the first week."

"There was more than one?"

"One a week, right through the end of the month."

"Who were they made out to?"

She didn't answer directly. "They was just the usual handouts. I done it before for Mr. L., when he was too busy to be bothered. And Mrs. Lessing said specifically not to bother him about it, so I just went ahead and made them out."

"Janey authorized these checks?"

"Not her. The other Mrs. Lessing. His mom. She called to the office and said to give this boy a check for two hundred dollars if he come in. So I did. She called again the next week, and I done it again. Right through to the beginning of June."

"Did Lessing ever ask about these checks?"

"I mentioned them to him myself, first of June. You know—kind of kidding him about all the money he was spending on this one charity case."

"And what did he say?"

She shrugged. "He didn't say nothing right away. But later on that day he said everything was okay."

I got Meg Lessing's address on Sunset Avenue from Millie. It was a street in Highland Heights, just a few miles from Covington. Before leaving I asked Millie to whom Mrs. Lessing had wanted the checks made. I already knew, but I wanted to hear her say it.

"Well, I guess it don't hurt to tell you," Millie said. "His name was Tom T. Chard. I remember 'cause he always wanted me to put that 'T.' in the middle there. He seemed to get a kick out of that."

I'll bet, I said to myself. To Millie I said, "Did you tell Len all of this this morning?"

She nodded.

"He never asked about it before today?"

"Nope. Why should he? He didn't have nothing to do with that kid."

He didn't then, I said to myself. But he did now.

I thanked Millie for her help, got up, and went to the door. "Tell Len I need to talk to him, Millie. Tell him it's important."

She promised she would.

31

. . . .

It took me about ten minutes to get to Sunset Avenue, driving due west through the fringes of Covington, where the city dies off in blocks of Quonset liquor stores and the concrete plazas of used-car lots. I took Devou Park Road up into Highland Heights, winding through sun-streaked, rolling acres of parkland to the bluffs that ring the city.

Sunset Avenue was on the very top of the tallest bluff—an exclusive street with a spectacular view of the river and downtown Cincinnati. Unlike the upwardly mobile French Quarter houses of Riverside Drive, the homes on Sunset were older, more typically suburban, less fashionably modern ranch and split-level, fed by cement curlicues of driveway and surrounded by great green swatches of well-tended lawn. These were homes meant for family living—kids, dogs, pool parties, outdoor barbecues with the neighbors. The good life, circa 1960. Riverside was strictly eighties—self-contained, glitzy, easy to keep.

The differences struck me as significant, but then I was thinking about the difference between Meg Lessing's world and that of her son—a difference she'd seemingly discovered months before his death. There was no other way to account for the series of two-hundred-dollar checks she'd authorized to Tom T. Chard—in Lessing's name. They might have been blackmail payoffs; they might have been hush money. But I had trouble believing that it was just good old-

fashioned generosity that had impelled a woman like
Meg Lessing to fork out two hundred bucks a week to
a kid like Tommy T.

The fact that she'd paid the boy off with Lessing's
funds, rather than using her own checkbook, was also
interesting. It could have been that she'd wanted to
disguise the extortion plausibly as charitable contributions—to protect herself and her son as well.

The woman's home was midway down the block, a
split-level with a redwood deck in back, sprung above
the cliff face like a diving board. The house proper was
sided in cedar shingles that had weathered to a pow-
dery pewter gray. A long driveway ran up to the front
door, cutting across a bluegrass lawn whipped by the
lazy loops of sprinklers. A plaster Negro jockey nestled in the grass near the front door, stiff and wild-eyed
as a jackrabbit.

I parked the Pinto in the shade of a carport and
walked up to the stoop.

I knocked, and a moment later Meg Lessing opened
the door. Behind her a short hall opened onto a stark,
sunlit living room, furnished gravely in ladder-back
and linen. The room ended in a fieldstone wall with a
fireplace built into it. Above the fireplace was a large
painting of the woman standing with her hand on the
shoulder of a burly silver-haired man—Meg Lessing
and what I took to be her husband, Tom. The man in
the portrait was smiling flaccidly, like a well-oiled
drunk.

"I need to talk to you, Mrs. Lessing," I said to the
woman.

She stared at me defiantly with those cold, stony
eyes. Her fingers played nervously with the gold cross
around her neck.

The past few months had clearly taken their toll on Meg Lessing, just as they had on her daughter-in-law. She'd lost a good deal of weight, enough for it to show in her face and figure. But she hadn't lost her bearings, as Janey had. She looked every bit as tough as she had on the night I'd first met her—the night that her son's bloody car had been found in the Terminal lot. It gave me pause to think that she'd known about Chard at that very moment—and hadn't said a word to me or to the police. In fact, she'd wanted me out of the case—wanted to "keep it in the family."

"You have a lot of nerve coming here," the woman finally said in a clipped, angry voice. "I thought Don made it clear that your services weren't needed."

"You mean regarding Tom Chard?"

She didn't even blink when I mentioned the name. "Yes. If that's the boy you told Don about."

I shook my head. "C'mon, Mrs. Lessing. You didn't need me to tell you who Tommy Chard is."

"I don't know what you're talking about."

"Yes, you do. And if you don't want the police crawling all over your son's life again, you'll quit lying about it."

"I'll call the police myself," the woman snapped. "And have them arrest you for trespassing."

"Do that, Mrs. Lessing, and you'll give me no choice. I'll have to go to the newspapers about the two-hundred-dollar checks you gave Chard back in May."

For a split second the woman looked shocked, but she recovered immediately. "You wouldn't dare do that. You have no proof that I signed anything."

"You told Ira's secretary, Millie, to sign checks made out to Chard. I have Millie's testimony to that effect."

"The girl's mistaken," she said flatly.

I stared at her in amazement. "What is it that Chard's holding over you? It must be pretty terrible."

"I have no idea what you mean."

And suddenly I knew, just by looking at her—her sportive face, her iron-stiff posture, her country-club clothes, her spartan house, her husband's portrait on the wall, her world on Sunset Avenue—that Chard didn't need anything special to intimidate and manipulate Meg Lessing. All he'd needed was the truth about Ira.

I said, "When did Chard come to you, Mrs. Lessing? When did he tell you that your son was a homosexual?"

The woman's face turned beet-red and her mouth— her whole face—started to tremble. "You bastard," she said in a deeply wounded voice. "You insufferable bastard. How dare you stand there—in front of my house —and make those kinds of accusations about me and my family? What do you know about me? What do you know about my life? You have no right to be here at all, you son-of-a-bitch!"

It was pointless to say that I hadn't blamed her for Ira's problem, because that was obviously the way she read it, as if her son's guilt were also her own guilt. And maybe it was so. Maybe she'd been living with a burden of guilt since Lessing was a boy. If Ira actually had been abused by his father, if Meg had known or suspected and done nothing about it . . . to keep face, to avoid scandal, to keep the marriage intact. It was a commonplace scenario, but it made me feel bad for the woman, standing there red-faced and biting back tears of rage. It made me feel bad for her in the same way I'd felt bad for Trumaine—when he'd failed to rescue Janey.

"Mrs. Lessing," I said in a conciliatory voice, "I have no desire to hurt you or your family."

"Then why don't you leave us alone?" she said bitterly.

"You know why," I said. "You've been paying extortion to Chard. This spring. Perhaps this summer. And you're about to do it again."

"No," she said, shaking her head.

"Mrs. Lessing, I *saw* Len meet with Tom Chard in Lytle Park last night. I know that Chard is expecting a lot of money."

She clapped a hand to her mouth so violently that it made her wince. "You saw?"

I nodded. "If you're planning to pay him off, Mrs. Lessing, it's not going to do any good. Chard will keep coming back. Hasn't he done that already? And sooner or later someone else is going to get hurt. Do you want Len's death on your conscience?"

She winced again, but I didn't let up.

"Don't you understand that Chard may have killed your son? He may have killed Ira?"

She shook her head until she almost went cross-eyed. "No, no, no, no. He didn't do that. There is no evidence like that."

"Then why shield him?" I said. "Why pay him extortion?"

The woman slumped a little, leaning back heavily against the doorjamb. "Because of the other one," she whispered. "So he won't testify for the other one."

"For Carnova?" I said, confused. "What could Chard say in Carnova's defense?"

But I knew the answer before I'd finished asking the question. I knew it without looking at the woman's flushed, shame-filled face.

"About the beat-freak business." I said it for her, feeling it fully, feeling her terror and embarrassment and disgust.

She didn't say anything. I don't think she could have spoken if she'd wanted to.

"You found out this spring?"

She nodded, almost imperceptibly.

"Chard came to you?"

She nodded again. "He had pictures," she said in a nauseated voice. "Polaroids."

"Christ," I said.

"What was I supposed to do?" the woman said, staring at me with naked bewilderment. "You can't . . . believe such a thing. But the pictures . . . I paid him. I didn't tell Ira. How could I tell Ira?" Her face contracted with pain and tears began to roll down her cheeks.

"Ira found out?"

"That stupid girl," the woman said, brushing savagely at her tears. "That Millie—she told him. Ira came to me one afternoon. I didn't . . . the subject wasn't mentioned. At the end of the afternoon Ira told me that I needn't worry about Mr. Chard any longer. And I understood that he didn't want me to authorize any more checks. That was the only time he ever alluded to this thing."

I could tell that she was parsing the conversation, that whatever else had passed between her son and her —whatever guilt or recrimination—was being left out of the account. But in spite of the omissions I couldn't help thinking that that conversation with Mom must have stayed on Ira's mind: those checks, that painful afternoon—maybe the day he'd torn out of his calendar—spent talking to his mother, talking around the terrible truth.

"You didn't pay any more money to the boy after the meeting?"

"No, Ira . . . handled it on his own," she said stiffly. "That was how he wanted it. I respected his wishes." The woman's mouth curled into an angry frown. "Of course if he'd had someone else to share this with, a helpmate who was strong enough to lean on . . ."

Her voice died out and she glared at me.

It was obvious that Janey had been right—that Mrs. Lessing did blame her for what had happened to Ira.

"You didn't make out two more checks to the Light-house Clinic early in June?"

"No," the woman said firmly. "I didn't see Chard again until long after Ira's death. He swore that he had nothing to do with the murder."

"You believed him?" I said incredulously.

"Why would he kill Ira when Ira had been giving him all that money?"

She had a point, although Lessing had given money to Terry Carnova too. "Did Chard say why Carnova had done it?"

"He said that the other one was angry with him—because of his relationship with Ira. He said that Carnova felt . . . jilted."

32

. . . .

Before I left I asked Meg Lessing how long Len Trumaine had known about the extortion.

"I told him yesterday," the woman said. "Before that he didn't know a thing."

"Why did you decide to tell him?"

"Because of you, I think," the woman said with some bitterness. "The boy, Chard, was getting nervous. He thought someone was following him, trying to entrap him. He wanted to leave town. Yesterday morning he called me. He asked for a great deal of money—thousands of dollars. I couldn't . . . I needed Len to get that kind of money. Naturally, Len was suspicious, especially since you'd just talked to him that afternoon about the boy. I felt I had no choice but to tell him the truth."

There was a falsity in her voice—not in what she said, but in the way she said it, as if confiding in Trumaine wasn't a matter of circumstance but of design, as if she'd turned to him because she knew she could manipulate him with guilt and make him do just about anything. Len the errand boy.

I said, "Len paid him the money last night?"

She shook her head, no. "He wanted to talk to the boy first—to confirm what I had told him. You see it wasn't any easier for him to believe than it was for me."

I could imagine Trumaine's dismay. And I could

also see him volunteering to do the dirty work. He
would have seen it as his lot.

"When is the payoff to be made?" I asked.

"Sometime tonight, I think. Len didn't tell me all of
it."

I backed away from the door. "I've got to find him."

"Mr. Stoner," the woman called out.

I looked over my shoulder at her. I thought maybe
she was going to ask me to look after Trumaine. Instead, she said, "What I've told you . . . it will remain
confidential?"

"Don't worry, Mrs. Lessing," I said, trying to mask
my disgust. "It will."

I drove back down the hill to the city, straight to the
plastics factory. Trumaine's Volvo was gone, and that
worried me.

I parked on the street and went in the front door.
Millie didn't smile at me this time, and that worried
me too.

"What's wrong?" I said.

She bit her lip. "Mr. T.'s on the warpath. Guess I
shouldn'ta opened my big mouth."

"You told him that you'd talked to me about the
checks made out to Chard?"

She nodded. "I thought you said you was gonna try
to help him."

"I am, Millie."

"Well, he sure didn't act that way. He cussed me like
a Marine and went piling on out of here."

"Where did he go?"

"I don't know." Millie gave me a wounded look.
"What the heck's going on, Mr. Stoner? Why is everybody so riled up?"

"It's a long story, Millie. But if it's any consolation, you did the right thing telling me."

"I sure hope I did," she said uncertainly. "But I ain't sure. I ain't sure what none of this means."

I drove from the plastics plant to Riverside Drive on the off chance that Trumaine had gone back to Janey's house. But I didn't see his Volvo on the street, and when I got up to the terrace I found Janey all alone, sitting in a cane chair, sipping a glass of whiskey and staring out at the river. She was wearing a blue silk dress and her face was carefully made up, but the expression on it was sullen and abstracted. She didn't look drunk yet, but she was obviously working on it.

"Mr. Detective," she said in her flat voice. "What can I do for you?"

"I'm looking for Len? Is he here?"

"Was. This morning." She took another sip of whiskey. "We had some business to transact at the bank. He needed my signature, I guess, to withdraw money from Ira's account. I can't think of why else I was invited." She looked off in the distance. "He must be having some trouble with the business. I don't begrudge him the money. He's been very good to me—all my life. I was more than happy to pay him off."

It was an odd thing to say, and she said it oddly, as if she had nothing other than money with which to repay Trumaine's devotion.

"You don't know where he is now, do you?"

"I think he went to the Court House—to have some documents notarized."

"All right," I said. "If you see him later this afternoon, tell him to call me."

I started to go.

"Mr. Stoner?" the girl said.

I looked back at her.

"Something's going on, isn't it?"

"No," I said, "I just need to talk to Len."

Janey laughed disgustedly. "You're lying. So was Len. It's all lies now. Lies and excuses and looking the other way."

"Did Len say something to upset you, Janey?"

She laughed again. "Oh, Len would never do anything like that. He loves me too much to upset me."

I ducked my head embarrassedly. "He *does* love you, Janey."

"Yes?" she said defiantly. "And what am I supposed to do about it? Love him back? I can't. I never could. He knows that, but he won't . . ." She tossed her head, looking away from me. "What are you supposed to do with a love that you have no use for, Mr. Stoner?"

I didn't say anything. There was nothing to say.

She turned back to me with a tragic look on her face. "I don't want anything bad to happen to him. I just don't want him to . . . I tried to tell him today, but he didn't hear me. He didn't understand. He thinks I'm holding a grudge against him for the past. He doesn't understand, Mr. Stoner, that I never held the past against him. It never was that. I just don't feel about him the way he feels about me."

I'd been there myself, God knew. Where Trumaine was with Janey. And I could feel for him. For her too.

"And now I'm afraid he's going to do something stupid," she said, sinking back into her chair with a fearful look. "Something dangerous."

"What makes you say that?"

"The way he was acting. The way he was talking

about . . . about the past and about Ira." The girl's face lit up weirdly and her voice rose, as if she wanted to scream. "Something *is* happening! And he won't tell me, and neither will you."

"He doesn't want to hurt you."

"What could hurt me more than not knowing?" she asked. "Please, Mr. Stoner. Tell me what's happening."

I didn't know what to answer. Like everyone else in the Lessing case, I'd lost my taste for the truth.

"It's not for me to say, Janey," I said, knowing the words were wrong as I spoke them, seeing the girl sink beneath them, as if that were *her* lot—to be betrayed by those she trusted. "But I promise you—no harm will come to Len. Tomorrow he can tell you. And if he won't, I will."

But the girl wasn't stupid and she wasn't reassured. She stared at me with that damaged look of betrayal on her face and said, with absolute certainty, "Something's going to happen. Something awful."

33

. . . .

What Janey said was true—something *was* about to happen, and despite my promise to her, I wasn't at all sure I could control it. Not without help. I felt concerned enough to stop at a phone booth on my way to the Court House and call Jack O'Brien at his office.

It was well past noon, and I figured that O'Brien had talked to Art Finch by then—and gotten an answer about Chard.

As it turned out he *had* talked to him, but the answer wasn't what I'd expected.

"He said no dice, Harry," O'Brien said unhappily.

"For chrissake, why not?"

"He says there's no evidence to connect Chard to the deaths. But that's not the real reason. The real reason is that he doesn't want to pick Chard up as a suspect in an aggravated homicide right before the Carnova trial. It would give me something to use in Terry's defense —and I *would* use it, believe me, no matter what Terry says."

"Did you tell the kid about Kitty?"

"Not yet. I was busy all morning with Finch and the D.A." He laughed bitterly. "They both acted like they'd never heard of Tommy T."

"They've heard of him, all right," I said with disgust. "Finch has known for months that Chard was tied to Lessing. Christ, he had the same leads I had. He just didn't follow up on them."

"Can you prove that?" O'Brien said.

"You mean can I prove a conspiracy to obstruct? Not without the testimony of a whole bunch of people who aren't willing to appear in court."

"Are you including yourself in that group, Harry?"

I said, "What do you mean?" Although I knew exactly what he meant.

He said it for me: "You were a witness to Terry's first confession."

"We still aren't sure what happened on the night of Lessing's murder, Jack."

But it didn't persuade me anymore. And it sure as hell didn't persuade O'Brien. "You're going to let Terry fry, aren't you, Harry? After all this horrible crap, you're going to let the kid go to the electric chair and let the other one go free."

"I'm going to find Chard," I said to him. "Count on it."

"And then what?" O'Brien said. "The cops won't arrest him. No one's left to testify against him. We probably couldn't even get a grand jury interested—not without the sort of proof that only you can supply. It's up to you, Harry. It's entirely up to you."

"I'll handle it," I told him.

When I finished with O'Brien I drove over to the Court House. It was lunch hour and the lobby was deserted. I went up to the commission offices on the second floor, looking for Len. The young woman I'd met in Don Geneva's office—the pretty blonde named Gloria—was standing at the head of the hall thumbing through a manila folder. She smiled at me as I walked by, and I smiled back at her.

"If you're looking for Don, he just went out to lunch," she said.

"I'm looking for Len Trumaine. Do you know him?"

The girl nodded. "He was here about twenty minutes ago."

"Where?"

"In Ira Lessing's office. I gave him my key so he could get in." The girl combed her blond hair back from her face. "You know Mr. Lessing was a good friend of his."

"I know."

"I didn't see Mr. Trumaine leave. Would you like to take a look?"

I nodded. The girl folded up her legal work and led me down the hall to 210. She took a key ring from her pocket and opened the door.

Len wasn't inside.

"I guess he must have left, after all."

"You think I could nose around in here?"

The girl said, "Sure. If you need me, I'm down the hall in 226."

When she left I sat down behind the desk. I didn't know what I was looking for—or what Len had been looking for. But I examined the desk thoroughly. Nothing appeared to have been moved. The picture of Janey was still on the right-hand side; the picture of Meg on the left. The calendar was still open to July 4. The stuff in the top drawer was untouched.

It occurred to me that Trumaine had simply stopped there to mourn his friend. The blow that Meg Lessing had delivered had to have hurt him deeply. And the night with Chard couldn't have been any better. The thing that frightened me was that he'd apparently personalized the situation beyond any debt he owed to Lessing. From what Janey had said, Len was viewing Chard not only as a threat to the family but as a threat to his own manhood. By confronting Chard he was going to redeem himself in the eyes of the girl, redeem the past. It was sad craziness, but it seemed to be real enough to him.

It got a lot more real to me when I opened the side drawer and found the chrome-plated revolver missing from its plush box.

I stood up and went down the hall—to 226. The girl read the troubled look on my face—I wasn't trying to disguise it.

"What's wrong?" she said with concern.

"We've got a situation here," I said nervously. I started to tell her about the gun, then realized there was no way to explain it without explaining the whole thing. And there wasn't time enough to do that.

"Is it Mr. Trumaine?" she asked.

"Yeah." I took out one of my cards and put in on her desk. "If you see him, or if you talk to Geneva and he's seen him, please give me a call. I've got an answering service and I'll check in on the hour."

"It sounds serious," the girl said, paling.

"Believe me. It is."

34

. . . .

I spent the rest of that afternoon searching for Len. I went back to Sunset Avenue, to Meg Lessing's house, but the woman took one look at me and slammed the door in my face. I guess I couldn't blame her. I'd forced the truth out of her, and I doubted if she'd ever forgive that—no matter who ended up in jeopardy.

From Sunset I drove back to Riverside Drive again, but Janey had either passed out or gone somewhere else, because no one answered the door. After that I tried the plastics factory—without any luck. And the Court House. I even tried the bar at Mike Fink's riverboat, but Trumaine wasn't there.

Every hour I called the office for messages, but there weren't any. Two or three times I thought about calling the CPD. But each time I balked at turning Len over to the cops, especially since I knew he was carrying a gun and was in the mood to use it.

As the day wore on the heat and my lack of sleep began to take its toll. By four o'clock I was almost stuporous with fatigue and soaked with nervous sweat. If I hadn't been so concerned about finding Trumaine, I would have gone back to the office and caught a few hours sleep. But I didn't trust myself to sleep. Not without knowing where and when that meeting with Chard was scheduled to take place.

So instead of sleep I stopped at a Frisch's along the riverfront and drank coffee until I was so wired I couldn't hold another cup. The fatigue was still there, but my head buzzed above it. I was suddenly full of hot ideas—foolish, dangerous ideas. The kind of things I wouldn't even have considered in a normal state. I could stake out Lytle Park, which is where the last meeting had been. And when Chard showed up I could take him before Len had the chance to do something stupid.

I wasn't thinking about how dangerous trying to take Chard on my own could be when I was in a worn-out funk, with my reflexes out of commission and my mind half asleep. I just wanted to settle it before someone else was killed.

And then a phone rang somewhere in the back of the noisy restaurant, sharp and clear as a cymbal strike, and I thought, *The hell with it—I'm calling the cops.*

I got up and went to a phone booth in the lobby off the dining room, sat down on the little metal seat, and started thumbing through the book, looking for the CPD's homicide number. I went through it twice before I realized it was a Kentucky directory. I was about to let the book drop on its chain when it occurred to me that there was one other obvious place where I hadn't looked for Len Trumaine. I'd never been to that place, but it was certainly worth a shot. I paged through the directory again until I found what I wanted, then left the restaurant and drove to East Fifth Street in Covington.

According to the phone book, that was where Trumaine lived—at 717 East Fifth. I knew I was on the right track as soon as I turned onto the block. Trumaine's red Volvo was parked on the street at the foot of a long, sun-drenched flight of stairs leading to an apartment complex.

It was a four-unit hillside apartment house built in terraces so that each apartment was set back from and above the one beneath it, like the tiers of a stadium. According to the mailboxes, Trumaine's apartment was the third in the row. I dragged myself up the steps to the third tier. A wooden gate opened off the stairway, leading to a fenced cut-stone patio. I walked across the patio to the front door and knocked.

A moment passed and, to my relief, Trumaine answered.

I could tell from the pink, puckered look of his eyes that he'd been crying. I could also see that he'd been drinking heavily.

"I don't want to talk to you," he said, trying to shut the door.

"I don't give a shit what you want, Len." I pushed him out of the doorway into the hall.

Between the booze and everything else that had happened that day, Trumaine was in no mood to be shoved. He took a swing at me—a roundhouse right. Drunk as he was, it didn't connect with anything but air. I pinned his right arm and shoved him into the wall, twisting his left arm behind him.

"Quit it!" I said fiercely. "I didn't come here to hurt you, but I damn well will if you don't start acting like a man."

I could feel him stiffen up.

"Let go of me," he said in a drum-tight voice.

I released his arms. He stood there for a moment, face to the wall, then slowly turned around. His fat cheeks were red, his eyes wet with embarrassment. He passed a hand through his short brown hair and pursed his lips savagely.

I said, "Are you going to throw another punch?"

"I'm thinking about it."

I shook my head. "Jesus Christ, Len. I could take you apart, do you know that?"

He glared at me. "So?"

"So how the hell do you think you're going to handle a kid like Chard—all by yourself?"

Trumaine dropped his eyes. "I don't know what you mean."

"The hell you don't," I said, jabbing his chest with my hand.

He winced and jerked his head up, staring at me angrily.

"You're going to sober up on coffee," I said to him. "And then we're going to talk."

"There's nothing to talk about. I'm going to handle this thing on my own. I don't want your help."

"Len, if you pull a gun on that son-of-a-bitch, he'll kill you. And don't bother to tell me that you don't have a gun, because I've been to Lessing's office."

"You followed me?" he said, looking outraged.

"Yeah, I followed you, you dumb bastard. I've been trying to find you all afternoon—before you got yourself killed."

He leaned back against the wall. "I . . . I haven't decided what I'm going to do."

"Then let's talk about it."

I followed him down a short hall to a living room of buff leather and oiled walnut. There was a conversation pit in front of a mantel, with a framed FSA photograph of a dust-bowl Oklahoma shanty hung above it.

There were other photographs on the walls—some of them familiar, some of them obviously taken by Trumaine himself. He'd never mentioned photography as a hobby, but judging by his pictures, he had a good eye, a sad eye. All the photos were of abandoned places —tract houses with "For Sale" signs in their yards, long rows of decaying tenements in the west end.

There was a picture of Janey above a desk—the only picture of a person I saw in the room. But it was Janey as a child. Before Lessing had happened to her. Perhaps before her own tragedy had happened. A golden-haired little girl of twelve or thirteen. Heartbreakingly pretty, and smiling with a life that I'd never seen in her.

When Trumaine saw me looking at the photo, his face flushed. He picked a tumbler full of scotch up off a coffee table and drank it, then sat down heavily on an armchair, as if the whiskey had knocked his legs out from under him. He sat there for a long time, staring off into space.

"I don't have anything to say to you, Harry," he finally said. "There's nothing left to say."

"Why? Because your friend wasn't the man you thought he was?"

Len's lip curled in disgust. "He wasn't a man at all," he said with such bitterness that it shook me. "He was all an act—a trick done with mirrors. The last ten years of my life . . . they don't mean anything. And Janey . . ."

His mouth trembled and he put both hands to his eyes.

I didn't say anything.

After a while he dropped his hands.

"I've got to put an end to this nightmare," he said in

a heartbroken voice. "Or I'll lose her too. I'll lose it all —everything that matters to me."

"You think killing Chard will stop it?"

"He's evil," Len said through his teeth. "He's an evil person. He's going to destroy us if I don't act. He's going to destroy Janey."

"How, destroy Janey?"

"If I don't pay, he's going to tell her about Ira!" he said in an agonized voice.

"She's already guessed some of it, hasn't she?"

"She doesn't *really* know," Len said. "She feels guilty, because of the newspaper articles, because of the rumors. But she hasn't seen the Polaroids—she hasn't seen the truth."

"Where are the Polaroids?"

He pointed toward the desk, then turned his head away as if he couldn't bear to look. "In the top drawer of the desk. Chard gave them to Meg four months ago."

I went over to the desk and opened the top drawer. And there on the pen dish was one of Tommy T.'s Polaroids of Ira Lessing—one of the vilest photographs I'd ever seen.

Lessing was crouching on a bed, naked. There was a studded belt around his neck, pulled so tight that Lessing's agonized face had turned purple and his eyes had rolled back in his head. Tommy Chard was kneeling on the bed behind him. In one hand he was holding the free end of the belt, jerking it taut. His other hand was buried inside Lessing—up to the elbow. The ferocious pleasure in Chard's eyes had to be seen to be believed.

Involuntarily, I slammed the drawer shut. For a moment I couldn't look at Trumaine. And when I turned around he couldn't look at me.

"Chard told Meg that he wants money—a lot of money," Trumaine said, staring at an empty corner of the room. "If he doesn't get the money, he'll show those pictures to Janey—to the press. I met with him last night to arrange it."

I didn't tell him that I already knew about his meeting with Chard—I didn't want to make him any more upset than he already was.

"I withdrew the money this morning, out of Ira's account. But after talking to Janey . . . I can't go through with it."

"Why?"

"Because Chard will keep coming back, threatening her, holding Ira over her like a sword, until he's bled us dry. And then he'll probably tell her anyway—just for the sheer, vicious thrill of it."

"Maybe if *you* told Janey the truth . . ." I said softly.

Trumaine stared at me, horrified. "Are you crazy? God, you saw that picture. It would destroy her."

"She may be stronger than you think."

"She's not," Trumaine said firmly, almost angrily. "She needs to be protected. She always has."

But I knew better. I knew that Janey's dependency was the only bond left between them. The girl had tried to tell him so herself that very afternoon. But he'd heard it as a challenge—to do a better job this time, to take better care of her and win back her love. A love he'd never really possessed.

For a moment I felt so bad for the man that I didn't know what to say: He was willing to die so that he could keep pouring Janey's drinks, holding her hand, and counting her pills.

"When are you going to meet with Chard?"

"Late tonight. I'm going to meet him up in Lytle Park. And then . . ." He stared at me—his schoolboy face frightened but determined.

"You're going to kill him."

He nodded grimly.

"No, you're not," I said to him.

"Why shouldn't I?" Trumaine said.

"Because I am."

35

I made Trumaine coffee in the small kitchen off the living room. After drinking a few cups he'd sobered up enough to think clearly about what I'd said.

"Why would you do this thing, Harry?" he asked with genuine confusion. "Why would you risk your life for me?"

"The bastard's had a hand in two deaths. Three if you count Lessing."

"He says not," Len said, sipping at the coffee. "He claims he wasn't involved in Ira's murder."

"He talked to you about it?"

"I asked him. He said he saw Ira earlier that night—at a bar called the Ramrod. Apparently Ira . . . he didn't normally go into those bars. But that night he was so upset, he went into the place, looking for Chard."

Lessing had told Janey that there was going to be trouble before he'd left on the night of the Fourth. "Did Lessing tell Chard what had upset him?"

Len nodded. "Those two checks to the clinic—the ones you found on Ira's desk. Ira was very angry about them and wanted to know where Chard had gotten them."

That was a piece of information I'd spent a lot of time trying to find—unsuccessfully.

"And where had he gotten them?" I asked.

Trumaine looked down at the floor. "Chard says from Janey."

I stared at him with surprise. "She knew?"

Len shook his head. "Chard claims she didn't. He claims he got the checks by accident."

"Accident?"

"He was supposed to meet Ira at the Court House that afternoon—to get some money." Trumaine gave me an embarrassed look. "Apparently he'd been extorting money from Ira for some time—from Ira and from Meg, God help her. But that afternoon Ira stood him up. He canceled his appointments for the day. Chard got so pissed off that he went to the house on Riverside Drive. He didn't actually tell me this, but I had the feeling that he went there hoping to find Janey —hoping to throw a scare into Ira by showing up at his doorstep when his wife was around. But Ira wasn't home, just Janey. As an excuse Chard told her that Ira had promised to give him the usual handouts for the clinic, and Janey apparently wrote two checks in Ira's name."

"Janey told me she didn't write the checks—that she didn't know Chard."

"Why would she remember his name?" Len said. "Christ, the kid was there for two seconds. And the last few months haven't exactly been kind to Janey."

"If it was all so innocent, then why did Lessing get upset?"

"Don't you see?" Len said with a gruesome smile. "Ira thought Janey knew. I mean he couldn't ask her outright—that would have been impossible. But when he discovered she'd signed those checks, he couldn't be sure that she hadn't found out about . . . about the pictures. He couldn't be sure that Chard wasn't extorting money from Janey in the same way he'd been extorting money from Meg."

It did make a horrible kind of sense.

Ira had had his meeting with Meg on the third of June—that meeting where his secret was laid bare before his mother. And then the very next day Marty Levine had called him from the clinic with the news that Chard had showed up with two more checks that Ira knew nothing about. He must have called Meg immediately, and when Meg told him that she knew nothing about the checks, some fear or premonition must have prompted him to call Janey. When his wife told him that she *had* signed the checks, it had shaken the poor bastard to the core. He could have spent the whole month brooding about it, wondering if Janey knew but afraid to ask her, afraid to broach the topic. Hell, even if Ira hadn't believed that Janey'd heard the truth from Chard, he couldn't ignore the fact that Chard had gone to her in the first place, that the kid had demonstrated that he *could* bring Lessing's world down around his ears anytime he wanted to.

Here was the source of the violent change in Lessing's behavior—the change that Carnova had told Jack O'Brien about. Maybe the man had just stopped caring what happened to him at that point. Or maybe, after a month of brooding, he'd decided to end it on that hot July night rather than go on living with the frightening uncertainty that Tom T. Chard had brought into his life.

I said, "Did Chard tell Ira how he'd actually gotten the two Lighthouse checks?"

"He says he tried to. But he claims that Ira was so worked up that he wouldn't listen to him. Eventually, Ira stormed out of the bar. Later that night Terry Carnova picked Chard up in Ira's car and . . . well, you know what Carnova said happened."

I stared at Trumaine. "You believe Chard?"

"I don't know," Len said after a moment. "I don't know what I believe anymore. The kid's obviously a liar. He could be playing games with me—protecting himself. But why would he kill a man he had wrapped around his finger—a meal ticket?"

"Maybe he saw Ira getting away from him," I said. "Maybe he realized that Lessing had had it with extortion, that he wasn't going to sit for it anymore."

"I'd like to believe that." Trumaine dropped his head heavily. "I loved that guy, Harry. I guess I still do. I mean the part of him that was good and sane and compassionate. But when I think about the other half —the tormented, soulless creature in that photograph —I'm almost glad he's dead."

"Give it some time, Len."

Trumaine laughed dully. "I don't have time. Chard isn't going to give me any time. Something's got to be done tonight. One way or another, it's got to be done."

"When is the meeting set for?"

"Three-thirty this morning."

I thought it over for a moment.

"You meet him at the park—with the money," I told Len. "Don't bring a gun. Don't do anything stupid. Just give Chard the payoff and let him go. I'll handle it after that."

Len gave me a long look.

"You're not going to do Janey any good by getting yourself killed," I said.

"I'm not doing her much good alive," he said softly.

"Look, whatever's wrong between you two is something you'll have to work out on your own."

"And if it can't be worked out?"

"Then you're going to have to live with it, Len. Just

like the rest of us do. But if you have any real feeling
for that girl, you won't put her through another nightmare. Or do you think she can survive your murder on
top of Lessing's?"

He flinched visibly, but all he said was, "I'll think
about it."

I went from Len's place back to the office. I knew I
was going to have to be clear-headed and strong to do
what I had to do late that night. I knew I needed sleep.
I lay down on the office couch, shut my eyes, and listened to the late-afternoon sounds of traffic coming
through the open office window. In a matter of moments I drifted off.

I woke up around eleven—woke up to darkness, like
a guy on third shift.

The night was still full of life. Traffic sounds, voices,
music from bars floated up from Vine Street. The
nightlife would begin to wind down in a couple of
hours. And a couple of hours after that I'd have my
meeting with Tommy T.

I walked down the hall and rinsed off in the john.
Glanced at myself in the mirror—at my weary, busted
face. I didn't look too long, though. I didn't want to
start asking myself questions.

When I got back to the office I went over to the safe,
opened it, and took out an oily chamois I'd kept inside
for years—since I'd been an investigator on Walker
Parsons's staff at the D.A.'s office. Wrapped inside the
oily cloth was a silencer made to fit a .45 automatic. I'd
taken it off a thug in the Sheraton-Gibson Hotel and
locked it away, oiled and unused. A souvenir with a
purpose. I'd never thought that purpose would arrive
for me. On that night I felt it had.

I cleaned the thing out with a gun rod and a pad soaked in Break-free.

I left it sitting on the desk, in the desk light, while I went down to the street—to an all-night coffee shop on Sixth—and had a sandwich for dinner. It was the first thing I saw when I got back. Heavy, chromed, snub, gleaming in the light like a drain pipe.

The Reds were on the Coast, playing the Giants— the tail end of another off season. I listened to the game for an hour or two and thought of my grandfather, who would keep box scores of each game during the summers, fanatically recording every out, as if he were keeping the casualty list of a distant war.

Around two-thirty the night noises outside my window began to die down. By three, all that was left were siren sounds, occasional hoots of drunken laughter, and the clip-clop of the carriage horses heading back to the barn on Central. I flipped off the radio, went over to the desk, picked up the silencer, and fitted it onto the barrel of my Gold Cup. The piece was too long for a holster, so I stuck it in my belt, around back, where a jacket would cover it.

I got a sports coat from the rack, put it on, turned off the desk light, and went out.

36

. . . .

It was five after three when I stepped onto the street. I
headed south to the underground garage, down Vine
to Fifth. There were still a few late-night types wandering the sidewalks. The heavy drinkers who close
the bars and the ones who stay for the company. Bums
with grocery carts full of ragged clothing, wheeling
their belongings down the sidewalks. In a half hour
they'd be gone—home or into the night. And then, if
Trumaine did what I'd told him to do, it would just be
me and Tommy T.

I picked up the car in the garage, circled around to
Fifth Street, and then to Lytle Place. I parked on
Fourth, directly across from the park. The ornate
facade of a residential hotel rose on my left, its canopied entryway dimly lit by brass lamps fixed to the
building. On my right the park grounds shimmered in
the moonlight—lawns and sidewalks turned silver, the
ginkgo trees powdered with the same silvery light.
There was no one moving around—no one I could see.

Reaching behind me, I took the Colt out of my belt.
There was enough street light falling through the
windshield for me to see the piece clearly—the blued
barrel with the thick chrome snout of the silencer on
the tip. I cocked it, locked it, put it down on the seat.

Around three-twenty a patrol car turned onto
Fourth. I ducked down in the seat as it cruised by.
Through the open window I could hear the amplified
static of its radio, and then the burst of the dispatcher's

voice sending out a call on Vine. The police car sped up, rumbling down Fourth.

As I straightened up on the seat I caught sight of someone in the rearview mirror coming down Pike Street at the east end of the park. I ducked again as he crossed Pike into the park grounds. When he plopped down on a gaslit bench I could see him clearly—Tommy T. His dirty angel's face looked nervous. But then there was a lot of money at stake, and he had to know how much Len hated him.

Hunched down on the car seat, I watched him through the rearview mirror. If I'd been a crack shot, I would have gotten out of the car, braced my arm on the roof, and taken him out where he sat. But I wasn't a good enough marksman with a pistol to pin it all on a seventy-yard shot in the dark. I didn't want to take the chance of rushing him, either—not when he was obviously expecting trouble. It was much better to take him by surprise, when he was feeling good and safe and rich with all of Ira Lessing's money loading him down.

I wasn't worried about catching him alone after the payoff. I wasn't even worried about taking him on my own. It was Len who worried me. The whole plan was predicated on Trumaine's doing exactly what I'd told him to do. If he screwed up—if he started feeling brave again, started feeling that need to redeem himself in Janey's eyes—he could get killed. And Chard could get away.

When I left his apartment I thought I had Len convinced that my way was the only way to ensure what he wanted—an end to Tom T. Chard's reign of terror. But hunkering down in that seat, sweating out the last few minutes before the red Volvo would round Pike

onto Fourth, I couldn't help wondering if I'd made a
mistake—if I shouldn't have tried to make the pickup
on my own. Chard knew my face, but it would have
taken only a moment to drive up to him and fire.

I stared nervously into the rearview mirror—at that
kid sitting in the gaslight, at the street corner across
from him. Two or three minutes passed—slowly. And
then I saw the red Volvo turn onto Pike.

The kid saw it, too, straightening up in the bench
and putting his right hand in his jacket pocket. I was
sure he had his razor there, that he was fingering it
nervously—ready to protect himself, ready to slash
and run if Len tried to double-cross him. I said a silent
prayer for Trumaine and held my breath as he turned
onto Fourth, coasted down to the gaslit bench, and
came to a stop beside Tom Chard.

For a moment Chard didn't move. He looked both
ways, up and down the block. He looked behind him.
Then, very slowly, he got to his feet and went around
to the passenger-side door of the Volvo. He glanced to
each side again and opened the door. He still had his
right hand in his coat pocket as he got in.

I couldn't see inside the Volvo through the rearview
mirror. All I could see were the headlight beams of the
car knifing through the darkness, and the plume of
exhaust coming from the tailpipes of the idling engine.
The car sat there for what seemed an eternity, although it couldn't have been more than five minutes of
clock time. And then I heard the engine rev up.

I waited for Chard to get out. But he didn't get out.
Instead the car started down Fourth.

"Jesus, Len," I said under my breath.

I hunched farther down on the seat as the Volvo

passed me. When it had gotten a couple of blocks ahead, I started up the Pinto and began to follow.

The traffic lights were all flashing yellow at that time of the morning. So there was no chance of losing Len at a stoplight. I watched the Volvo's taillights dancing in and out of the shadows of the tall buildings along Fourth. At Vine a taxi cab coasted in between Len and me, but I could still see the Volvo clearly enough to keep track of it.

We went all the way across town, all the way to Central Avenue, before the Volvo came to a stop. The taxi cab went on ahead, turning right onto Central and heading uptown. I pulled over to the curb a block and a half behind the Volvo, doused my headlights, and squinted to catch a glimpse of what was going on inside Len's car. But I couldn't see anything at that distance except the silhouettes of two heads.

Perhaps Chard had gotten scared. Perhaps he'd feared a trap. Perhaps he'd ordered Len to drive around to shake a tail. Whatever the reason, the trip across town wasn't part of the plan. I knew that if they kept going, I could lose them. The entrance to the expressway was right across Central from where Len had parked. If they got on the interstate, it wouldn't be easy to follow—not if I intended to hang back. Even at that hour of the morning there'd be enough traffic on 75 for the Volvo to get lost in it. And I could come away with nothing.

I thought about gunning the motor and pulling up alongside the Volvo. I thought about cutting in front of them before they got on the entrance ramp, forcing Len off the road onto the berm. I thought I was a goddamn fool not to have shot the bastard when I first spotted him.

And then the passenger-side door of the Volvo opened, and Chard got out.

He was grinning his evil little grin, but he didn't look nervous and he didn't look toward me. He half saluted Trumaine, slammed the door shut, and jogged across West Fourth to the south side of the street. Trumaine started up the car and drove off, across Central onto the expressway.

It all had happened so quickly, I didn't have time to feel relieved. I watched the kid closely as he sauntered down Fourth toward the Plum Street corner. His windbreaker had large pockets, and I could tell from the way he kept patting those pockets that Trumaine had given him the cash.

Chard got to the corner of Plum and walked south toward Third. I saw him stop midway down the block and duck into an alcove of a bank building. He stood there for a long time—his upper body in shadow, his legs just visible in the moonlight. And I suddenly realized why he'd had Len drive him across town. Chard had caught a ride to his favorite corner, to his pickup spot. Maybe he was counting his money in that alcove, maybe he was catching his breath. Or maybe he'd gone to that corner to do business—to cap the evening by working over some poor slob like Ira Lessing.

The longer Chard stood here, the more certain I became that he really was waiting for a car to cruise by. Any car. Anybody. He was feeling mean and brazen and invincible, with enough money in those coat pockets to take him anywhere he wanted to go. He obviously didn't need the cash from a john. What he needed was the thrill—the ugly thrill of making one more Ira Lessing crawl and beg and plead for him to stop. One last chance to make himself feel big at another man's expense.

I was going to give him that chance.

I watched a car cruise by, slowing up a little at the Plum Street corner before speeding off, and I knew exactly how to go about it.

I was going to cruise Tommy T. Pick him up, like Lessing had. It was dark on Plum, dark enough so that Chard couldn't see much of my face inside the Pinto—especially if I turned up the collar of my sports coat and hunched down on the seat. If I kept the car on the west side of Plum, where the shadows were heaviest, there'd be no reason for him to think that I was anyone other than some poor sap looking to get hurt. If he bit and came over to the car, I'd have the gun on him as he got inside. If he didn't bite, I'd get out of the car and take him where he was standing—right there on the dark, empty street.

. . . .

37

Turning up my coat collar, I started the engine, flipped on the headlights, and pulled out onto Fourth. It was just half a block to Plum. I wheeled left onto the dark side of the street and slowed to a crawl just as I came up to where Chard was standing.

Hunched down in the seat, with the silenced gun in my right hand, I pulled over to the curb, flashed my lights four times—using Carnova's code—then turned off the engine. After a moment Chard stepped out of the alcove. I kept my face hidden as he crossed in front of the Pinto. He came directly over to the driver's-side window—a knowing smile on his lips. The car window was unrolled. Still grinning, he ducked his head inside.

As soon as he saw me his eyes popped. But by then I had the barrel of the silenced gun pressed against his mouth, right up against that nasty grin. I grabbed his hair with my left hand and pulled his head all the way through the car window.

"You can't do this, man," he shrieked through his mushed-up mouth.

"Oh, yes, I can, kid. Tonight I'm the law."

"Fuck you!" he shouted.

He threw his right hand up, and I saw the razor catch the moonlight. Even though I had him by the hair, with his upper body halfway inside the car, he managed to bring the razor through the window and flail at me. For a second all I could see was that flashing blade and the kid's wildly bucking head and shoulders. It was as if I was being attacked by an animal. I felt the razor ripping through my right coat sleeve, cutting into the flesh of my arm. I jerked back and the gun went off with a flash and a muffled pop, straight up into the roof. The car filled with gun smoke.

I took my finger off the trigger and started using the gun like a sap, clubbing at Chard's flailing arms and jerking head while trying to keep my grip on his hair. But in the tiny space of the car I couldn't get any leverage. He kept slashing at me, cutting me again on the right hand before I managed to hit him hard enough on the temple to knock him out.

I saw his eyes roll back, and then his upper body went limp. The razor dropped from his hand onto the floor of the car. I pushed Chard's head back out of the car window, and his body slid to the pavement.

For a second I just sat there, breathing hard. There was blood up and down my jacket—his and mine. He'd been tugging so hard that I'd pulled out a handful of hair. I wiped the blood and hair off my hand, wrapped a handkerchief around the deep cut on my right hand, and got out. The kid was lying on the pavement by the driver's-side door, moaning and holding his bloody head with both hands. I reached down and grabbed him by the back of his windbreaker, dragging him around to the passenger side of the Pinto.

"Wha' the hell?" he said groggily.

Opening the passenger-side door, I reached inside the glove compartment and took out a pair of cuffs. I flipped Tommy T. on his stomach and cuffed his hands behind him, then tossed him onto the seat, slamming the door behind him. Before getting back in on the driver's side, I took a close look up and down the street. No one had driven by. There was no one else visible on the block.

I put the car in gear and drove slowly away.

In a few minutes we were on River Road, heading west toward Saylor Park. It started to rain. A slow drizzle that made the headlights glint on the dark, oily tarmac. To the left I could see the river lights guttering in the dark current. On the right the white clapboard houses of Anderson Ferry gradually gave way to gravel pits and open lots.

Chard had come around by then. He sat still on the seat, head bowed and bloody. "I didn't do nothing to you," he said bitterly. "I didn't."

"What about Kent and Kitty, Tommy? What about Ira Lessing?"

"I didn't do none of that, either."

"Yeah, you were just an innocent bystander."

"It was Terry that done Ira. Not me."

"You're lying, you little cocksucker."

The kid bucked, like I'd jolted him with a prod. If he could have gotten the razor, he would have attacked me again. "I ain't no cocksucker," he screamed. "I ain't no fag."

I laughed. At that moment in his life that was all he could think to say.

"Terry was the cocksucker," he said. "Terry was the faggot. Warming up to that rich-ass son-of-a-bitch. Calling him his dad. I told him I could get in that man's crack anytime I wanted to. But he thought he had something special going. So I just had to show him —thinking he's better than me, 'cause he had some faggot that treated him nice."

I glanced over at him. "You took Lessing away from Terry?"

"Shit, yes, I did. Ain't my fault Terry was too stupid to see what was happening—until Lessing told him. That's what set Terry off. Hearing his big-deal lover boy tell him he wanted some of what I'd been giving him."

"How do you know that?"

For just a second he looked perplexed. "How do you think?" he finally said. "Terry told me when he picked me up that night. Crying and moaning and talking like he done killed his father—when all he done was kilt some worthless faggot."

I slapped the kid with the back of my hand. Hard. Right on his mouth.

He spit blood on the dash. "You take these cuffs off," he shrieked. "I'll hurt you so bad, you won't ever forget it."

"Is that how you used to talk to Ira?"

"Yeah." He started to laugh wildly. "I made him cry like a girl. I hurt him so bad he couldn't walk."

He laughed for a long while, until he was sick with laughter. When he'd laughed himself out he sat back hard against the seat.

"You got the gun, so you think you're better than me. But you ain't better than me. You ain't nothing. Ain't no man better than Tom T. Chard."

A few miles outside of Saylor Park I turned off the highway onto a gravel access road that led down to the river. Chard hadn't said a word for some time. He knew what was coming, and he was holding out against it.

The road ended in front of a broken slab of concrete

that had once been the foundation of a house. A little rise surrounded it, falling away in a field of weeds, broken pop bottles, and junk auto parts to a grove of maples along the riverbank.

It was close to five by then, and the dawn had just begun to turn the eastern sky violet. But the river and the maple grove were still deep in night. I left the headlights on to light the way, then pulled Chard out of the car and pushed him over the rise down toward the trees.

The handkerchief around my hand was soaked with blood. There was blood dripping down my arm from the cuts on my shoulder. But I wasn't thinking about my wounds; I'm not sure I was thinking at all.

"I ain't gonna die," Chard said as he walked down to the bank. "You can't kill me. Ain't no man gonna kill Tom T. Chard."

When we got to the maple grove he began to cry. He stood there facing me, his bloody face lit up by the headlights, and pleaded for his life.

"Don't do this, man," he said, sobbing. "Don't do this to me. I got money. Lots of money. You can split it with me." His eyes lit up. "You can have it all!"

"I don't want the money."

"What do you want!" he screamed, falling to his knees in the muck.

"The truth about Lessing."

He looked up at me, his hair plastered with gore. "I was there, okay?" His face contracted and he groaned like an animal. "He was just a fag, man."

"Is that what you told Terry?"

He looked up at me with a touch of defiance in his streaming eyes. "Yeah. That's what I told him. He was just a fag. Just something to whop on."

I shot him in the head.

He fell back in the weeds—what was left of him.

I took the cuffs off his wrists, took the money from his jacket. Rolled his body over to the bank, filled the coat pockets with stones, and pushed it in. I dropped the silencer in the river too.

I got back in the car and drove up to River Road. There wasn't enough light for anyone to identify the car, even if there'd been someone around to see it. I pulled onto the highway and started east, back to town.

I stopped once at a roadside shelter, west of Delhi near the river, and cleaned the blood off the seats and dash with some rags I used to wax the car. I tossed the rags and Chard's razor in a barrel full of trash, pushing them down deep in the can and covering them over with junk. I used a spigot to wash out the cut on my hand and rewrapped it in a fresh handkerchief. There wasn't a thing I could do about my shoulder or my clothes until I got back to the apartment.

By then the dawn had begun in earnest, turning the sky white and the air a pearly gray. I sat down on a park bench next to a swing set and stared at the river, going to gold in the dawn. I sat there for quite a while. Then I got back in the car and drove home.

38

. . . .

I didn't phone Len for a couple of days. I didn't talk to anyone.

On Monday, Carnova's trial began—and ended. It took all of thirty minutes for him to plead guilty before a panel of judges. Sentencing was scheduled for the following week, pending a mitigation hearing.

On Sunday morning I went to the Justice Center to talk to Carnova. I didn't expect him to agree to a conference, but he did. Maybe Kitty had mentioned me to him. Maybe O'Brien had. Whatever the reason, he recognized my name.

The meeting took place on the fifth floor, in the visitor's room. He sat behind a glass shield. His face had changed. It looked old now and weary. His voice had lost its wild young edge too. He sounded tired, resigned, as ready for death as an eighty-year-old man.

"You was a friend of Kitty's, wasn't you?" he said after we sat down across from each other.

"I knew her."

The boy swallowed hard. "She shouldn'ta never cared about me. I told her I wasn't worth it. She shouldn'ta cared."

I didn't say anything.

"I just wisht I coulda gone to her funeral."

"They wouldn't let you?"

He shook his head. "I got stabbed in the mess hall. Had to stay in the infirmary."

I ducked my head. "It's been tough for you inside."

"I deserve it," he said in his old self-dramatizing style. "Every bit of it. Ain't enough they can do to me now. I kilt my dad and I kilt my wife."

"You had some help," I said bitterly.

He knew exactly who I was talking about. "Tommy didn't do no more'n what I woulda done had I been in his shoes. He's just looking out for himself, like he always told me to do. Got to look after yourself first. Ain't no one else gonna do it for you. Just get to the head of that line and take what you can."

Tom T. Chard's philosophy of life.

"He had a . . . relationship with Ira Lessing, didn't he? Your friend Tommy."

The kid's face turned a little red. "It weren't no 'relationship.' He mighta seen Ira with me sometimes, I guess. Ira was *my* friend."

"That's not true, is it, Terry?" I said softly. "Lessing had been going to see Chard for some time, behind your back."

The kid didn't answer me. He just sat there with a wounded, angry look on his face.

"You didn't know about that, did you?" I said. "Not until that night, when Ira told you."

"He didn't tell me nothing," the kid said angrily. "There weren't nothing to tell. Ira was *my* dad." The kid got up from his chair. "I ain't gonna talk to you no more."

He signaled to a guard and walked out of the conference room.

But I sat there for a while longer, thinking about Terry and Ira and Tom Chard. In its own way the murder had been a crime of passion—or passions. Crippled by his compulsions, Ira had courted his own death. And Terry had delivered it to him, with

Tommy T. urging him on. Urging him to act like a real man—to give his lover what he really wanted, what he'd come to Tommy to get.

High on T's and B's, furious over being betrayed by his friend and his lover—on his birthday, no less— Terry had started pushing Ira around, beating him the way Tommy did it. Only Terry was no expert; he wasn't Tommy T. He was just a jealous lover who was deliberately goaded into losing control of his violent temper. And who had lived in guilt and remorse ever since.

Guilt, remorse, and that one little secret he obviously intended to carry to the grave. The secret that had kept him from mentioning Chard to the cops. In the Byzantine world of homosexual hustlers, where the hustlers were "real men" and the johns were just fags to be used and discarded, Terry had committed the unpardonable sin of caring for a client. And then Tommy T. had come along and shown him just how stupid that affection was—just how easily it could be stolen away by a "real man."

It had started to rain when I came out of the Justice Center, a cool, gentle rain that chilled the air. In a week or two that burning summer would finally end and it would be fall.

I picked up the car in the Justice Center lot and drove slowly down Main Street. I knew what I had to do, but it was going to be hard as hell to explain it to Len and to Janey—why I was going to testify about the doctored confession at the mitigation hearing.

I picked up speed on the expressway and headed for

the Brent-Spence and Covington. With any luck I'd find both of them at the house on Riverside Drive. Then we could sit down and talk, about Ira and Terry and Tommy T.

FREE FROM DELL

with purchase plus postage and handling

Congratulations! You have just purchased one or more titles featured in Dell's Mystery 1990 Promotion. Our goal is to provide you with quality reading and entertainment, so we are pleased to extend to you a limited offer to receive a selected Dell mystery title(s) *free* (plus $1.00 postage and handling per title) for each mystery title purchased. Please read and follow all instructions carefully to avoid delays in your order.

1) Fill in your name and address on the coupon printed below. No facsimiles or copies of the coupon allowed.

2) The Dell Mystery books are the only books featured in Dell's Mystery 1990 Promotion. No other Dell titles are eligible for this offer.

3) Enclose your original cash register receipt with the price of the book(s) circled plus $1.00 per book for postage and handling, payable in check or money order to: Dell Mystery 1990 Offer. Please do not send cash in the mail.
Canadian customers: Enclose your original cash register receipt with the price of the book(s) circled plus $1.00 per book for postage and handling in U.S. funds.

4) This offer is only in effect until April 29, 1991. Free Dell Mystery requests postmarked after April 22, 1991 will not be honored, but your check for postage and handling will be returned.

5) Please allow 6-8 weeks for processing. Void where taxed or prohibited.

Mail to: **Dell Mystery 1990 Offer**
P.O. Box 2081
Young America, MN 55399-2081

NAME_____

ADDRESS_____

CITY_____STATE_____ZIP_____

BOOKS PURCHASED AT_____

AGE_____

(Continued)

Book(s) purchased:_____

_____

_____

I understand I may choose one free book for each Dell Mystery book purchased (plus applicable postage and handling). Please send me the following:

(Write the number of copies of each title selected next to that title.)